ANGEL IN THE SQUARE

CINDY KIRK

WAVERLY
HOUSE

CHAPTER ONE

Balancing the cake box in one hand, Jenna Woodsen used the other to ring the bell of the nondescript house on Philadelphia's north side. Even though working here as a house parent could be challenging, Jenna would miss her weekend shifts.

The door flung open, and Keisha, a tall woman with an explosion of black curls and bright red lipstick, motioned her inside. "Sorry to keep you waiting. I dropped a plate in the kitchen and was cleaning up the mess."

"No problem." Though the rain was more of a heavy mist, not uncommon for April, the porch roof had allowed Jenna to stay dry while she waited. "Can I help?"

"All done." Once Jenna was inside, Keisha shut the door, then flipped the deadbolt.

Jenna glanced around. "Where are the girls?"

Last weekend, there had been six, all between the ages of 13 and 17. The number who lived here constantly fluctuated. Sometimes, because a girl was reunited with her family or because the caseworker had found a foster home willing to take one of the teens. And, rarely, it was because one of the girls aged out of the system.

"Misty and Denisha are in their rooms. Jubilee, Suri and Ella are in the living room. Violet—"

"—is right here." Violet, tall and slender with a mass of strawberry-blond curls and large blue eyes, smiled at Jenna. "You came."

Pleasure ran through the girl's words like a pretty ribbon.

"I told you I would." Jenna held out the bakery box. "What's an eighteenth birthday without a cake?"

Violet's blue eyes never left Jenna's face. "Letting you go isn't fair."

Jenna shot a quick glance at Keisha.

The woman immediately raised her hands. "Don't look at me. I didn't say nothing to nobody. I figured I'd leave that up to you."

Shifting her gaze back to Violet, Jenna cocked her head. "Do the others know?"

"Not yet."

"How did you hear?"

Violet lifted one thin shoulder, then let it drop. "Does it matter?"

Keisha chuckled. "The girl has a point."

Jenna let it go. How Violet had heard didn't matter. After tonight's birthday celebration, Jenna would tell the rest of the girls that her part-time position had been eliminated.

She could have let them figure it out when there was only one staff member on duty this weekend, not two. But she'd forged a bond with them, and they'd already experienced enough friends and family walking away without a backward glance.

Jenna's gaze slid from Keisha to Violet. "Is this a good time for cake?"

"The way I figure, it's always a good time for cake." Keisha chuckled and glanced at Violet. "How about you, birthday girl? Are you ready to get this party started?"

Violet grinned. "I am."

The two followed Jenna into the kitchen. They watched her

take brightly colored party plates and plastic forks from a bag she'd brought with her before lifting the cake from the box.

"Incredible." Violet stared, wide-eyed, at the gorgeous confection that boasted a star charm rising above the cake on a swirl of LED lights.

"You're a rising star, Violet." Jenna's voice filled with emotion. "In my heart, I know you're destined to do big things."

"Thank you, Jenna." A soft look stole over Violet's face. "Not only for the amazing cake, but for the support you've given me."

Impulsively, Jenna gave her a quick hug. "Happy, happy birthday, sweet Violet."

When Jenna stepped back, she found Keisha staring.

Jenna raised a hand to her cheek. "Do I have something on my face?"

Keisha shook her head and smiled. "It's just when I see the two of you together, I can't get over how much you look alike."

This wasn't the first time someone had made that observation. Though their hair and eye colors were different, Jenna had to admit her facial features and Violet's were very similar.

"Of course we look alike." Violet shot Jenna a wink. "She's my big sis."

Jenna chuckled. Instead of going by the traditional "house parent" moniker, staff members at this group home were referred to as "big sisters."

An hour later, after the singing, candle-blowing and everyone enjoying delicious cake from one of the finest bakeries in Philadelphia, it was time for Jenna to leave.

Keisha had to make sure everyone's chores were done and that the girls were ready for school tomorrow. Everyone except for Violet, who'd graduated midterm.

The only thing left was for Jenna to let the other girls know she wouldn't be coming back. Most acted like they didn't care. Jenna knew differently.

After saying good-bye to each of them, Jenna turned to Violet. "Walk me to the door?"

She soon stood alone in the entryway, facing the tall girl on the brink of womanhood. A face full of freckles made her appear younger, but her eyes, deep and knowing, said she'd already seen more than most.

"You'll soon be on your own." Jenna met Violet's gaze. "I want you to remember that you're strong and smart and capable of doing whatever you set your mind to. I firmly believe your future holds much happiness."

Violet settled a hand on Jenna's shoulder and met her gaze. "I believe yours holds the same."

"You've got my number. If there's ever anything I can do for you—"

"I'm certain our paths will cross again." Without warning, Violet wrapped her arms around Jenna and squeezed tight. "For now, take care of you."

～

On the drive home that night, Jenna pondered Violet's words and wondered if her worry over the loss of the part-time income had shown.

Jenna was the sole support for herself and her great-aunt Rosemary, so the money she'd earned at the group home had been a buffer for the unexpected. Her full-time position as an RN caregiver for Cherise Menard covered their regular expenses, but Jenna had liked the cushion.

The next few days passed quickly. On Friday, when Jenna arrived at her day job, it struck her that once this shift ended, she had the entire weekend free. Perhaps she and Rosemary could go to the Philadelphia Museum of Art tomorrow. Or maybe visit the nearby Amish country and pick up some Dutch apple jam or a shoofly pie.

Throughout the day while caring for Cherise, Jenna happily considered the options. After giving the day's report to Timothy, who would cover the evening shift, Jenna was nearly to the door when Britta, the housekeeper and one of Jenna's good friends, called her name.

She turned, surprised when the petite brunette hurried over to her. "Mr. Menard wants to speak with you."

Although Michael Menard had been the one to initially interview and hire her, she'd had little contact with him since.

That had been fine with Jenna. While she genuinely enjoyed Cherise, there was something about the woman's husband that she found off-putting. He was arrogant, which she expected from someone in his position, but it was the hint of mean in his eyes that had her keeping her distance.

Not that he'd ever sought her out. Until now.

Britta gestured. "He's in the study."

Jenna knocked on the open door, and he motioned her inside.

"Close the door," he ordered in a brusque tone.

Her heart tripped, and she clasped her hands together to still their trembling. She told herself she had nothing to worry about. Cherise liked her, and Mr. Menard could have no complaints about the quality of the care she gave his wife.

Dressed in one of his expensive suits, with his short hair holding just enough gray to give off a distinguished vibe, Michael Menard was the picture of a successful businessman.

With a hand sporting perfectly manicured nails, he gestured her to a leather visitor's chair. "Have a seat."

Once she did, instead of sitting behind the ornate executive desk as he had when he interviewed her, he sat on the edge of the desk. He was so close she could smell the not-so-subtle scent of his cologne.

It was a popular fragrance, an expensive one, but not one she liked. Right now, the smell of it had her stomach lurching.

When he said nothing, Jenna offered a bright smile. "Britta said you wanted to see me."

He appeared puzzled, then he waved a dismissive hand. "Ah, yes, the housekeeper."

Falling silent, he appraised her with cool blue eyes.

Jenna shifted in her scrubs, which were a soft raspberry. As Cherise didn't want to feel as if she were in a hospital or health center, her caregivers were instructed to wear high-end scrubs in any color except white or gray.

When Jenna had left the house, Rosemary had told her today's scrubs color made her eyes look like pools of melted chocolate. The comment had made her smile.

Right now, she didn't feel like smiling. Something in Mr. Menard's gaze had her shifting uneasily in her seat.

"Cherise told me you lost your second job." A look of sympathy crossed his face. "That has to be quite a blow. I'm sure you count on the extra income."

Normally, Jenna wouldn't have mentioned the loss of the group-home position to Cherise, but the woman, a former civic activist, loved listening to Jenna's stories about the girls. Of course, Jenna always carefully omitted names and any identifying personal information.

When Cherise had asked about the girls earlier in the week, Jenna had felt obligated to tell her what had happened.

Never in a million years had she thought that Cherise would bring the situation up to her husband. Or that he'd be interested enough to mention it.

"Budget cuts." Jenna offered what she hoped looked like an unconcerned shrug. "It happens."

"Still, you don't have a husband or boyfriend to fall back on."

Despite finding the comment with the underlying question a bit personal, Jenna told herself the man was only showing concern. "No. No husband or boyfriend. Just me and my great-aunt, Rosemary."

The man's lips lifted ever so slightly. "That's what I thought. Cherise has mentioned your aunt, too. Must be quite the burden, having her depend on you for everything."

"My great-aunt is not a burden." Jenna fought to keep the offense from her voice.

"Of course not. I simply meant that it must be hard, financially speaking. Especially now."

"I appreciate your concern, but Rosemary is waiting for me." With great effort, Jenna resisted glancing at the door. "If that's all—"

"I like you, Jenna. You seem like a bright girl. You clearly care about your aunt and," his eyes scanned her body, "yourself. I get the impression ensuring your aunt's well-being is important to you. Am I right?"

Jenna nodded. "That's right."

"Good. Because I have a way for you to earn extra cash. It's not something I'd offer to just anyone." He leaned closer to her and dropped his voice to a conspiratorial whisper. "Plus, I think it's the kind of thing a girl like you will like." He offered her a smile that reminded her of one she'd seen last year in his campaign ads, then named a figure. "Interested?"

Jenna's wariness was replaced by excitement. "Yes. I mean, possibly. What would it involve?"

Her smile fell away as he told her in explicit terms what she would be doing to earn that money.

Bile rose in her throat as she pushed back her chair and stood. "I'm not interested." But when she turned toward the door, his hand closed around her wrist in a steely grip.

"Not so fast."

Before she knew what was happening, he jerked her against him. "Let me give you a sample of what you'd be missing."

With one hand still locked around her wrist, his free arm snaked around her like a vise as he crushed his mouth against hers.

She struggled, but he had a good hundred pounds on her and a tight grip.

When he finally released his hold on her wrist to squeeze her breast, Jenna seized the moment. Grabbing the first item she could lay a hand on, a paperweight on the desk, she slammed it against the side of his head.

He stumbled back, raising his hand to his temple. When he lowered it and saw the blood, he let out a roar. "You goddamn bitch."

Jenna didn't wait to hear more and fled.

Wade Spahr, Mr. Menard's assistant, stood in the foyer, talking on his cellphone. He glanced up in mild annoyance as she rushed past.

Once out of the house, Jenna sprinted to her car, jerked open the door and jumped inside. She locked the doors before peeling off in the direction of home.

The apartment building where she lived was in sight when her phone rang. Jenna pulled into her parking spot and glanced at the screen. *Britta*.

"Hello." Jenna's voice shook. No surprise, as the rest of her body currently had the shakes.

"Jenna. I need to warn you—"

"If it's about Mr. Menard being a perv, I already know."

"It's worse than that. Mr. Menard is saying you assaulted him."

"I didn't assault him! He's the one who assaulted *me*. I hit him in self-defense." The tears Jenna had held in check all the way home slipped down her cheeks. "If I hadn't gotten away, I think he would have…"

Jenna's voice thickened, the realization of what she'd narrowly escaped hitting her full force.

"Oh, Jenna…"

"It's over." Taking a deep breath, Jenna let it out slowly and felt herself steady. "I'm going to speak with the agency and let them know what happened. I can't go back."

When Britta said nothing, Jenna added, "No matter how much I like Cherise, I can't work in that house, Britta. Not with him there."

"There's more, Jenna." Britta hesitated. "After you left, I overheard him talking to Mr. Spahr. The door was shut, but he was so angry he was practically screaming. Mr. Menard plans to pin the thefts on you. He's going to say that he walked in on you taking the jewels from the safe in his office and that you struck him when he tried to detain you. Mr. Spahr will back him up."

Jenna brought a hand to her head, which had started to spin. "Are you talking about Cherise's jewels?"

"Yes."

Several months earlier, Cherise had reported to police that over a hundred thousand dollars' worth of family jewels had been stolen. Thankfully, the rest of the gems had been locked away in the safe in her husband's office.

"If they charge you, it will be a felony."

"I didn't take anything." Jenna's voice rose, then cracked.

"I know you didn't. You know you didn't. But who will the police believe? Especially if Mr. Spahr corroborates what Mr. Menard said and says they caught you in the act." Britta's voice held a warning edge. "I heard him call the police and request an officer be sent over."

"I didn't take any jewelry," Jenna repeated. "He assaulted me. The only way I could get away was to hit him with that paperweight."

"It will be his word against yours. Even if I tell them what I overheard, Mr. Menard will say you and I are friends, and I'm just covering for you." Resignation filled Britta's voice. "Who do you think the police will believe? The important city councilmember? Or you?"

∾

"I can't believe you took a sabbatical from work so we could take a road trip." Rosemary, a handsome woman with deep-set blue eyes and a gray braid hanging down her back, gave a happy sigh. "Just taking off in a car and driving with no particular destination in mind reminds me of my youthful adventures."

Jenna slanted a smile at her great-aunt. "It'll be fun."

Once she'd gotten her emotions under control, Jenna had considered how to spin getting the heck out of Dodge, er, Philadelphia. The last thing she wanted was to worry her great-aunt. Rosemary had a weak heart, and doctors had advised Jenna to help her avoid stress, not bring it home to her.

Rosemary wasn't easily fooled, but she'd believed Jenna when she'd said she'd been saving money from her second job so they could have this vacation. And she hadn't blinked an eye when Jenna told her to make sure she took whatever she wouldn't want to leave behind in case they found the perfect spot and didn't want to leave.

The six months of living expenses that Jenna had set aside for a rainy day had been withdrawn from the bank. If the possibility of being charged with a second-degree felony punishable by ten years in prison and a twenty-five-thousand-dollar fine didn't qualify as a rainy day, Jenna didn't know what would.

When Rosemary had brought up Cherise, Jenna's heart had given a little ping. She'd assured her aunt that the Menards could get by just fine without her.

Wanting to get as far away from Philadelphia as quickly as possible, Jenna took Washington Avenue on her way to I-95. She slowed to stop at a light. That's when she saw her.

The thin girl, carrying a duffel with a cross-body strap, wore a hoodie that was no match for today's brisk wind.

Jenna pointed, her tone reflecting her shock. "That girl on the sidewalk is Violet."

"Violet from the group home?"

"Yes."

While they watched, Violet moved close to the curb and stuck a thumb in the air.

Jenna frowned. "She's hitchhiking."

"That's a dangerous thing to do these days." Concern filled Rosemary's voice.

At any other time, Jenna would have immediately pulled over and picked her up. But did she really want to draw Violet into the mess that was her life right now? If the police stopped them, could Violet be charged with aiding a criminal simply for being in the car?

Rosemary touched Jenna's arm. "You can't allow a stranger to pick her up," she said urgently.

No, Jenna thought, she couldn't. Ignoring the blare of horns, Jenna wheeled the car across traffic and stopped at the side of the road.

Jenna lowered the window on Rosemary's side and leaned across her aunt as Violet stepped to the side of the car.

"What are you doing hitchhiking?" Fear had the question coming out sharper than Jenna had intended.

"Why are you running away?" Violet responded mildly.

"We're not running," Rosemary answered before Jenna could. "We're off on an adventure. Please get in. Wherever you're headed, we'll take you there."

"That's a generous offer," Violet said as she slid into the back seat, tossing her duffel to one side and fastening her seat belt, "considering you don't even know where I'm going."

"Doesn't matter."

Violet returned Rosemary's smile. "I'm headed to GraceTown, Maryland."

Jenna pulled her brows together. "Is that near Baltimore?"

"About fifty miles west."

"Why there?" Jenna asked, pulling back into traffic.

In the rearview mirror, she saw Violet shrug. "I spent some time there years ago. It's time to go back."

Rosemary smiled. "Jenna and I are going wherever the wind takes us. It sounds as if GraceTown will be our first stop."

"If you need a place to crash once we get there, I know of a house that's empty." Violet covered a yawn with her fingers. "Save you money on a motel."

Beside Jenna, her aunt's eyes lit up. "It's been a long time since I crashed anywhere."

Jenna thought of the money she'd taken out of her savings account that morning. Money that would go a lot further if they didn't have to pay for housing for a night or two.

"The place has been vacant for years," Violet added, obviously sensing Jenna's hesitation.

"How do you know this?"

"I know a lot of things." Violet chuckled. "Like, didn't I tell you we'd meet again?"

CHAPTER TWO

GPS took Jenna and her passengers to north-central Maryland in a little under three hours. Jenna would have preferred more distance between themselves and Philadelphia, but when they pulled up in front of a massive brick and stone Victorian surrounded by a spread of green, her heart gave a twinge of yearning.

"It's gorgeous." Jenna narrowed her gaze. "Looks pretty good for a house that's deserted."

"The owner hasn't been here in over five years," Violet told her. "He pays the utilities and for basic house and yard maintenance, but that's it."

"Why did he quit coming?" Jenna studied the house, liking the tall windows and turret on one side.

"Actually, Daniel Grace—that's the owner's name—lives in New York City. He inherited the home from his grandfather, but he's shown no interest in living here." Violet stepped out of the car. "All of his grandfather's stuff is still here."

Rosemary opened her door, but made no move to get out. She tipped her head back, studying the imposing three-story home. "This takes me back."

Violet smiled. "How so?"

"In my younger years, my friends and I used to crash in abandoned homes." Rosemary's expression turned wistful. "It was great fun."

"Your hippie roots are showing," Jenna teased.

"Life is meant to be lived with gusto." Rosemary got out. "And once upon a time, mine was." A flicker of sadness crossed Rosemary's face. Before Jenna could find words to comfort her, Rosemary shook it off and was back to her optimistic self. "I can't wait to see the inside."

Jenna wondered how they'd get in, but Violet simply plucked a large skeleton-type key out from under the front mat. It slid easily into the keyhole. The door creaked open, and the three strode inside.

The hardwood floors were covered with Oriental rugs. The walls, plaster with ornate crown molding, were painted in bold colors of sapphire blue and primrose. The stairway leading up to the second level boasted pineapple newel posts and intricate designs on the banister.

Jenna wandered into the kitchen, expecting to find it antiquated, but she instead discovered a modern kitchen designed to appear vintage. The freestanding dual fuel range in midnight blue and brass likely cost more than she made in a month working two jobs.

"This place is no crash pad," Jenna told Rosemary, recalling the crushed-velvet sofa and antique Tiffany light fixtures in the parlor. "Someone will care that we're here."

Someone, Jenna thought, like local law enforcement. Exactly who she didn't want sniffing around.

"It will be okay." Violet spoke softly.

When she rested her hand on Jenna's arm, through the fabric of the jacket and the sweater underneath, her touch sent a pleasing warmth, along with a curious energy, flowing through Jenna.

The tension gripping Jenna's body eased. Maybe it would be okay to stay. She and Rosemary hadn't slept much last night, as they'd been up late planning what to take with them and what to leave behind.

At thirty, Jenna could still get by on little sleep. But a seventy-five-year-old with a weak heart needed her rest.

"A storm is coming," Violet announced. "You don't want to be driving in the rain."

Jenna hadn't heard anything about a storm, but the sight of fatigue lines around Rosemary's eyes made the decision easy. "I'll pull the car around back where it can't be seen. We'll stay the night."

Violet nodded with approval.

Jenna parked the car in the garage, which was more like a carriage house, and brought their bags inside. By the time she shut the door behind her, rain had begun to fall in light drops.

Minutes later, the heavens opened, and the light pitter-patter on the roof became a roar.

"You were right about the rain." Jenna slanted a glance at Violet, who cast a pointed look in Rosemary's direction.

Jenna saw that her aunt had taken a seat in a rocker with a needlepoint seat and back. The older woman had grabbed a cotton throw from the sofa and wrapped it around herself.

"It was time to stop." Violet spoke in a low tone, not moving from where she stood in the hallway.

"That throw has to be dusty."

Violet shook her head. "Someone is coming in on a regular basis to clean."

"I'd almost rather the place be filled with clutter and dust." Jenna took another look around.

No dust. No clutter. Even the rail on the stairway appeared freshly polished. While they stood there, the furnace kicked on, telling her the home's old heating system had been converted to forced air.

An expensive, well-cared-for house. Definitely not the place to squat.

"Don't you like it here?" Violet asked.

Jenna's nose caught the clean, fresh scent of lemon wax. "I do. Who wouldn't? But this isn't an abandoned house, Violet. This place feels lived in."

"This house hasn't been a home for years."

Violet spoke with such certainty that Jenna might have been inclined to believe her, if they'd been talking about anything other than this house.

"There's no way you can know that for sure." Jenna gentled her tone, knowing the girl was simply trying to allay her fears. But Jenna couldn't afford to add breaking and entering to the charges that were likely already filed against her.

"Jenna." Violet touched her hand, her blue eyes glistening with reassurance. "We're safe here. Trust me when I say you're right where you're meant to be."

"I don't know what you two are gabbing about over there," Rosemary called out. "I hope it's about putting some food on the table. I'm starving."

Shaking off her unease, Jenna laughed. "It's not going to be anything fancy. How do cheese sandwiches, kale chips and fruit sound to you?"

As they'd hurriedly packed only what food they'd had in the apartment, the options were limited.

"Sounds wonderful." Rosemary expelled a heavy sigh and leaned back in the rocker.

"You know what would make this night extra wonderful?" Violet crossed the room and flicked a switch. The gas-lit logs in the fireplace began to glow. "It may just be April, but on a rainy night, there isn't anything better than a fire."

"Oh, Violet." Rosemary clasped her hands together. "You are so right."

As Jenna busied herself making the simple meal, eschewing

Violet's offer of assistance, she realized Violet and Rosemary shared many common characteristics.

They both had upbeat, cheerful personalities and were inclined to find the best in any situation. They also tended to be optimists. Which meant it fell on Jenna to be the realist.

Though she didn't think spending even one night in this house was smart, she also couldn't imagine driving on unfamiliar roadways in the rain after dark. Jenna assured herself they would get up early tomorrow and be gone before anyone knew they'd even been here.

With that now settled in her mind, Jenna set the dining room table with dishes she borrowed from the cupboards and called her two companions to eat.

"This looks very nice." Rosemary smiled at Jenna as she took her seat. "Thank you, Jenna."

"You're very welcome." Jenna was pleased to see healthy color in Rosemary's cheeks. Stopping had clearly been the right move.

After a few minutes, Rosemary smiled at the teenager. "Tell me about yourself, Violet. I know you recently had a birthday, but that's about all I know."

Violet followed the kale chips she'd been crunching on with a water chaser, then sat back in a chair that boasted feet carved to look like claws gripping a ball.

"I lived in a group home until last week, when I officially aged out of the system. You might say I'm alone in the world, but I don't feel that way." Violet cast a glance at Jenna and smiled. "So many good people have been there for me. Just like I'm there for them. Even after our short time together today, you feel like family, Rosemary."

"Families of the heart." Rosemary's lips lifted, and a distant look filled her eyes. "Back in the day, that's what my friends and I used to say. We might not be related by blood, but inside, where it really counts, we were family."

Violet nodded. "What's in our hearts is what binds us together."

"You said you used to live in GraceTown." Jenna tried to pull up in her memory exactly the words Violet had used, but decided that was close enough. "Did you live here with your family? Do you still have family here?"

"Anyone I knew back then isn't here anymore." Violet took another sip of water, carefully placing the glass back on the coaster. "I remember this as being a special place."

"I read your file," Jenna pressed, just a little. "I don't recall any reference to you living in Maryland."

"You know how it is with records and files." Violet's lips quirked upward. "They're hardly ever accurate."

"But—"

"What are your plans now?" Rosemary asked Violet, interrupting Jenna. "Now that you're here?"

"They're pretty open." Violet pushed back her chair and stood. "Right now, I'm going to answer the door."

As Violet began the trek to the front of the house, the doorbell sounded.

Jenna's heart slammed against her chest. "Don't answer it."

Ignoring the directive, Violet disappeared from view.

Should they make a run for it? Jenna glanced at her aunt, who continued to eat, finishing off the last bite of her cheese sandwich, unaware of the danger.

There was no way Rosemary could make a run for it, and Jenna certainly wouldn't leave her aunt behind.

"Jenna, dear, what's wrong?" Rosemary asked. "You've gone white as a ghost."

"I, ah, I wasn't expecting company," Jenna stammered.

"The more the merrier." Rosemary smiled. "That's what we used to say when we crashed somewhere."

Jenna bet those hunted by the police hadn't felt that way.

But the voices mingling with Violet's didn't sound stern and authoritarian, but female, soft and pleasant.

For a minute, Jenna couldn't make out what was being said. Then a peal of laughter had the tense set to her shoulders relaxing ever so slightly.

"The rain stopped just as we drove up," Jenna heard a woman say as footsteps drew close.

"The forecaster promised it would be a brief, but intense, shower," another said. "They got it right this time."

"We have our first visitors," Violet announced, stepping into the dining room with two women beside her. She gestured first to one and then to the other. "This is Geraldine Walker and Beverly Raymond."

Geraldine and Beverly looked to be in their early seventies. Both women sported hair that held more gray than brown. Geraldine wore hers short, while Beverly's hair formed a soft coil at the nape of her neck.

"They brought apple pie," Violet added.

"That's so kind of you." Jenna crossed to greet the women, trying hard not to let her trepidation show.

Violet gestured to Rosemary, who now stood at Jenna's side. "This is Aunt Rosemary and my big sister, Jenna." Violet looked at Jenna. "Geraldine and Beverly look after the house for Daniel."

"Well, you're certainly doing an excellent job. It's lovely here," Rosemary replied, shining a warm smile on Beverly and Geraldine.

Beverly beamed. "Thank you. We're happy to do it. It's important to take care of these historic homes. As we started to say to Violet when she answered the door, Geraldine and I were at a card party down the block and saw the lights on in the house. We thought Daniel had finally returned to GraceTown, so we ran home to grab a pie and coffee and—"

"What brings the three of you here?" Geraldine, who had been studying the women politely, but intently, interrupted.

Before Rosemary or Jenna could say a word, Violet piped up. "Jenna and Daniel are going to be married."

Jenna gaped at Violet in shock. *What?*

Beverly gave a little squeal. "How wonderful! I hadn't heard the news."

Geraldine focused on Jenna with a curious intensity. "When's the wedding?"

Jenna threw a quick glance at Violet, who nodded imperceptibly, as if to say, *Go on, trust me.* "We, ah, we haven't gotten that far," Jenna stammered.

Geraldine's sharp-eyed gaze dropped to Jenna's left hand. "No ring?"

"A simple gold wedding band and love are all I need." Jenna spoke from the heart.

When Beverly blinked back tears, Geraldine reached over and squeezed her friend's fingers. "I believe love is all you really need, too."

"Jenna has never been one for being flashy," Rosemary advised.

"She'll make a beautiful bride," Violet decreed. "What do you say we have some pie and get better acquainted?"

In order to give herself time to settle, Jenna insisted the others sit while she made coffee.

"There's a carafe in the cupboard to the left of the stove," Beverly informed her. "Are you sure you don't want help, hon?"

"You brought this amazing pie. The least I can do is get the coffee going." In the kitchen, Jenna's hands shook as she got the percolator perking.

"Don't worry."

Jenna turned. She'd been so lost in her thoughts that she hadn't noticed that Violet had joined her. "I-I'm not worried. I just don't understand why you told them I'm engaged to Daniel Grace."

Violet shrugged.

"You also told them we're sisters." Jenna's gaze remained on Violet. "I don't like to lie."

It was what she'd been doing since they'd left Philadelphia—making Rosemary believe this was simply an adventure and not letting Violet know all she was risking by simply being with Jenna.

"At the group home," Violet reminded her, "you *were* my big sister."

The explanation didn't calm Jenna's unease.

"That's true enough, I guess." Jenna licked suddenly dry lips. "I need to tell you something, Violet. I—"

"Not now." Violet's gentle hand on her forearm brought a familiar flood of energy. "It will be okay. Just trust."

For some reason, the simple assurance had the fear that had held Jenna's body in a stranglehold easing.

"Where's our coffee?" Rosemary called from the dining room, sounding almost jovial.

"Coming right up." Jenna glanced at Violet. The girl's quiet confidence was just the boost Jenna needed at that moment. "You're certain?"

"Positive." Without hesitating, Violet went to a lower cupboard and pulled out a tray, then she opened an upper one and took out enough cups for everyone.

"How did you—" Jenna stopped herself. At the moment, she had enough to think about without wondering how Violet had such unerring direction. "Never mind."

Over rich coffee and thick slices of apple pie, Jenna discovered that the two friends lived together in a house that, while not in the neighborhood, wasn't far. The card party they'd been at was a semiregular occurrence.

"When we saw the lights, we considered pulling into the driveway right then," Geraldine admitted. "But we'd only had snacks at the party and were ready for something more substantial. Beverly had a roast in the Crock-Pot at home."

Jenna's heart picked up speed. "Does Daniel come here to visit often?"

"No." Beverly looked at Geraldine, who shook her head. "Daniel hasn't been here in ages."

"But we didn't know who else it could be," Geraldine added, eyes, as always, on Jenna.

"Besides, if it had been Daniel, we figured he must have just arrived, and we wanted to give him time to settle in." Beverly smoothly picked up the conversational baton and ran with it. "We had dinner, cleaned up the kitchen, then decided to stop by with the pie. I knew there wouldn't be any coffee in the house, so we brought that along as well."

"When Violet answered the door, I was struck dumb for a second." Beverly gave a little laugh.

"Believe me, that rarely happens." Geraldine offered Beverly an indulgent smile.

"She's right," Beverly agreed. "It's a rare occurrence."

They passed a pleasant half hour during which Jenna discovered that Beverly was a retired RN, while Geraldine had once been part of her family's automotive-service business. Geraldine laughingly told them that while her title had been office manager, she was often pulled into the garage to help out when they were shorthanded.

"I've always been handy with tools." Geraldine took a long drink of coffee. "I have three brothers. Put a wrench or a hammer in my hand, and I could run circles around them any day of the week. Of course, my mother would have preferred I stick with more ladylike pursuits."

Violet offered a supportive smile. "We have to be who we are."

"Exactly right." Rosemary gave a decisive nod of agreement. "My parents were very mainstream, I guess you could say. In the '60s I embraced the counterculture. Many of those today scoff at that era, but we did a lot of good. I still try to give back more than

I take and to be open to new and different ideas and ways of living."

Jenna knew that giving back more than she took was why Rosemary had reached the winter of her life with little savings. It was no exaggeration to say that even now, her great-aunt would give away the coat off her back if someone else needed it.

"If you're open to the new and different, you've come to the right place." Beverly leaned forward as if about to impart a great secret. "GraceTown is known for unexplained happenings."

Intrigued, Jenna set down her coffee cup. "What kind of things are we talking about?"

"Things that shouldn't make sense, but do," Beverly said, still not clarifying.

"Sometimes you have to accept the unbelievable," Violet murmured.

"Exactly right." Geraldine took a sip of coffee, then asked Jenna, "When will Daniel be joining you?"

The way Jenna figured, when in doubt, deflect.

"How well do you know my…" Jenna couldn't, just couldn't, bring herself to say *my fiancé*, so she simply went with, "Daniel?"

Geraldine smiled. "We've known him since he was a little boy."

"Oh my, yes, what a wonderful child he was." Beverly's face lit up, then her expression sobered. "While we've been happy to maintain his grandfather's house for him, Geraldine and I have never stopped hoping he'd return and make GraceTown his home."

When Geraldine opened her mouth as if to ask again when Daniel would be arriving, Violet stepped into the conversation.

"It's kind of cool, him being a descendant of the founder of the town and all."

"A blessing and a burden." Beverly cast a glance at her friend and received a nod of agreement. "Everyone expects more from you when you're a part of the most prominent family in town. Of course, as I'm sure you know, his parents moved to Connecticut when he was ten."

"Fred was the last Grace to live here." A look of sadness blanketed Geraldine's face. "He was a good man and a friend to us both."

"He was blessed with a long, full life." Beverly gave her friend's arm a squeeze, then shifted her attention to Jenna. "Once Fred passed, we hoped Daniel would return to GraceTown. As the years went by and the house remained empty, we began to worry he might sell. The fact that you're here tells us those fears were unfounded."

Jenna sipped her coffee, then set down the cup. "GraceTown seems like such a lovely place."

"Big enough for there to be plenty to do, but yet, we've managed to retain a sense of community," Beverly added. "I hope that once Daniel joins you, he'll see that and want to stay forever."

Jenna offered a noncommittal smile and forked off a bite of pie.

"That might not be for a while." Violet's comment had everyone's attention shifting to her. "Daniel is hard at work on his next book."

Geraldine leaned forward, excitement filling her eyes. "What can you tell us about it? I devoured the first."

"I'm afraid you'll have to wait to read it." Violet made a zipping motion across her lips. "Everyone around him has been sworn to secrecy."

By the time the women left, Jenna felt as if she were in the last leg of a marathon.

"I didn't know Daniel was an author," she murmured to her aunt and Violet as they stood on the porch and waved good-bye to the women.

"Have you been living under a rock?" Good humor took the edge from Rosemary's words. "His first book was extremely successful. There was plenty of hard-hitting, fast-paced action, but what impressed me was his characterization of Curtis. He did a stellar job of portraying such a clearly troubled person with compassion."

Violet nodded. "I've always believed that to know an author, you simply have to read their work."

Jenna shifted her gaze from Violet to Rosemary, since it appeared that both were equally well-informed. "Okay, so he had a megahit and is now working on book two?"

"Exactly right." Violet smiled. "Living and writing in New York City."

Expelling a relieved breath, Jenna smiled. "Which means it's unlikely he'll be visiting GraceTown any time soon."

"Which is a shame." Rosemary shook her head. "This house needs to be lived in, to be not just a house, but a home."

Jenna absently nodded. All that mattered was that, at this moment, Daniel Grace was in New York.

Which meant they were safe…at least for tonight.

CHAPTER THREE

Daniel sipped his drink and stared out over the crowd celebrating Jessica Tower's fortieth birthday. Jesy, a children's book editor, was a good friend of Daniel's girlfriend, Calista Evers.

The event, held at Penthouse 45 in Midtown Manhattan, offered food, drink and panoramic views of New York City and the Hudson River.

He and Calista agreed the selection of wines offered was robust and admired the elegant cake that graced a table adorned with candles and flowers.

"The icing on the cake is a bourbon whipped cream."

Daniel pulled his gaze back to Calista. "Seriously?"

Calista nodded.

"Then we definitely need to get a piece."

Though dressed simply in a red wrap dress, with her layered blond hair, which hung in soft curls past her shoulders, and strikingly beautiful face, Calista drew the eye. Daniel caught more than one man looking her way as they mingled.

Calista, intent on talking business, didn't appear to notice.

Normally, Daniel enjoyed socializing, but not when he was

struggling to get his latest book to come together. And not when practically every person he met this evening had asked how it was coming.

Calista, who was not only his live-in girlfriend, but his editor, had done most of the deflecting.

He knew that casualness was only an act. Lately, it felt as if every conversation they'd had, as if the *only* conversation they'd had, related to the looming deadline.

Daniel had kept telling her he was making progress on the book, hoping that if he said it enough times, it would be true.

"Why the frown?" Calista slipped her arm through his and smiled up at him. Despite wearing three-inch heels, the top of her head barely reached his shoulders. "Relax. Smile."

She'd been saying a lot of that, too, these days. Did Calista really believe that all she had to do was tell him to relax, and it would be so?

Daniel empathized. He knew the pressure she was under. The powers that be expected her to produce another blockbuster. The problem was, Calista couldn't work her magic until he gave her something to work it on.

Daniel knew what was holding him back. He desperately wanted every word to be perfect, and none of them was. He wanted the scenes to flow and the pace to be gripping, and it all felt flat.

"Is everything okay, Daniel?" Obviously conscious of those around them, Calista spoke in a low tone for his ears only. "You haven't seemed yourself all evening."

He hadn't wanted to come to the party, but he couldn't tell her that, not when he'd agreed two weeks ago to be her plus-one. The truth was, he was tired of playing the role of the successful author when he couldn't get his second novel done.

Right now, it felt as if he would never be able to make the story work.

Though he definitely wouldn't say that to Calista, he could

admit that the New York scene wasn't fueling his creativity. Not only that, he'd begun to feel that mixing the personal with the professional in their relationship had been a mistake.

"I'm ready for warmth and sunshine." Daniel took a sip of wine. "It's been a long winter, and spring isn't coming fast enough."

"My father has a place on Marco Island in Florida." Calista's expression brightened. "We could go there for a long weekend."

He could see her thinking—though, to her credit, she didn't say it—that maybe a change of scene would be the creative boost he needed.

Calista might be a trust-fund baby, but she was devoted to her career. It was that passion that had initially drawn him to her.

He wanted to tell her that the trip he'd been envisioning was for one, not two.

"What do you say?" Her hopeful smile tugged at his heart.

"I say, give your dad a call."

Jenna woke to sunlight streaming through lace-curtained windows. Outside, a bird sat on a long branch, singing its heart out. She stretched, unable to recall the last time she'd felt so rested.

Last night, when she'd finally slipped into bed, she'd feared she might toss and turn with worry and be unable to sleep. Instead, resting her head on the pillow was the last thing she remembered.

She smiled. She could get used to a leisurely lifestyle.

Rolling over, she glanced at the bedside clock. Ten o'clock. Jenna's eyes widened, and she jolted upright. Leisurely was one thing. Sleeping the day away was quite another.

She dressed quickly. After seeing both Violet's and Rose-mary's rooms were empty, she headed for the stairs. Halfway down, she heard laughter. Jenna smiled, recognizing Rosemary's distinctive, deep laugh. The other, tinkling like a silver bell, was Violet's.

They were on the front porch, a fact that had Jenna wanting to shoo them back inside and shut the door. Didn't they realize that sitting out there advertised that the house was occupied?

Of course, Geraldine and Beverly had appeared well connected, which meant news of their arrival had likely already spread. Pausing at the base of the stairs, Jenna felt her heart skip a beat. Could the news travel as far as the GraceTown police station?

The second the thought surfaced, Jenna reminded herself she was being ridiculous. Hadn't she gone online last night and searched *The Philadelphia Inquirer* for any recent articles concerning Michael Menard? Hadn't she set up a new email account and then a number of Google Alerts with any terms she could think of that would alert her when anything related to her situation surfaced?

There had been nothing about the assault or the jewel theft. More important, there'd been nothing about her. Mr. Menard might have contacted the police, but it appeared that, for now, any charges hadn't made the news.

Pushing open the door, Jenna stepped out onto the porch.

Rosemary turned in her chair. "Good morning, sleepyhead."

"Good morning to you both." Jenna crossed to where the two women sat, Rosemary on a wicker settee and Violet in a matching chair. Taking a seat next to Rosemary, she gestured to the coffee carafe. "Is there more in that?"

"Of course there is." Rosemary took the cup that Violet offered and poured. Handing it to Jenna, she smiled. "I nearly went upstairs to see if you were still breathing."

Jenna arched a brow, then took a long sip of coffee. Strong and hot, just as she liked it.

"I told her I'd know if you were dead." Violet, dressed in jeans and a graphic tee, flashed a smile. "I have a sense about things like that."

"Really?" Rosemary appeared impressed, though Jenna knew Violet was only joking.

"I can't recall the last time I had such a good night's sleep." Jenna took another drink of coffee and gestured with one hand. "It's so quiet here."

The apartment building that she and Rosemary had most recently called home was located at the intersection of two busy streets. Though Jenna had thought she'd grown accustomed to the sounds of traffic, sirens and drunken shouts, she realized now that she hadn't.

"We slept exceptionally well, too." Rosemary cut off a piece of cinnamon roll, placed it on a small plate and handed it to Jenna.

"This one," Rosemary jerked her head in Violet's direction, "was up at the crack of dawn. She'd already been to the bakery and brewed a pot of coffee by the time I strolled into the kitchen at seven."

Jenna bit into the cinnamon roll, and her taste buds heaved a satisfied sigh. While she was glad to have the tasty treat, she wasn't sure Violet being out and about was smart. She couldn't stop the frown.

"This is a lovely neighborhood," Rosemary offered, obviously misinterpreting the reason for Jenna's unease. "Very safe and quiet. A young woman walking alone is in no danger."

"Several of the neighbors were out. They seemed nice." Violet smiled. "They'd already heard that Daniel Grace's fiancée had moved in with her sister and great-aunt."

"I'm not sure it's wise to be so visible." Jenna took another bite of roll and chewed thoughtfully. She almost said, *Not when the police are on my tail,* but then she remembered the two didn't know about the incident with Mr. Menard.

For the best, Jenna told herself.

The way it stood now, if law enforcement did show up,

Rosemary and Violet could honestly deny having any knowledge that they were with a criminal. Not that Jenna was a criminal. She'd done nothing wrong. That knowledge was what really stung.

The two were now gazing curiously at her, as if expecting her to continue. "We're squatters."

"I prefer the term house sitters." Rosemary's eyes held an impish gleam. "Besides, who is going to object?"

"What about Daniel?" Jenna couldn't believe her aunt was being so obtuse. "Remember him? The owner of this lovely house?"

"The man hasn't been here for five years." Violet spoke in a matter-of-fact tone. "We're not hurting his property. Anyway, it isn't good for houses to be empty. You could say we're doing him a favor."

Violet snagged the last bite of cinnamon roll, popped it into her mouth and grinned.

She looked so happy today, with her spill of strawberry-blond curls pulled back from her face with a thin band. The band matched the salmon color of her shirt, which had a circle of words proclaiming Be Kind around a peace symbol.

Jenna remembered the conditions at the group home. This had to be like heaven to Violet. Still, was it smart for them to stay here? The decision weighed heavily on Jenna's shoulders.

Violet met her gaze. "Don't leave."

"Leave?" A startled look crossed Rosemary's face, and her voice pitched high. "We just got here. Who said anything about leaving?"

Violet's gaze never left Jenna's face. "Your niece is considering all options."

"I am," Jenna admitted.

"I want to stay." Rosemary's chin wobbled, then she lifted it in a stubborn tilt that Jenna had rarely seen. "I like it here. The house—and this town—has a cool vibe."

Jenna nearly smiled at the description, though it was accurate. The house and the town did have a cool vibe.

"If you leave, I won't be going with you." Violet's voice remained soft and low. "This was my destination, and now that I'm here, I will stay. At least for a while."

Violet was an adult. The agreement had been to bring her to the town where she'd once lived. But, according to her, she no longer had any friends or family here. If Jenna and Rosemary left town, what would happen to Violet?

And Rosemary—what kind of life could Jenna give the older woman she loved like a mother? Jenna knew that she and Rosemary would never find a place this nice with the limited amount of cash in her wallet.

"You should stay." Violet let the words hang in the air for several seconds before continuing. "At least for a while longer."

～

Their first week in the house passed quickly. The exploration of the town yielded a grocery store within walking distance with friendly staff and reasonable prices.

The way Jenna saw it, the more they could keep her car with its Pennsylvania license plate off the road, the better. Neither she nor Violet minded walking, especially since spring had come and stayed.

Every night, Jenna checked the internet for Michael Menard news and found nothing. It was beginning to feel as if she could finally let out the breath she'd been holding.

When a lawn care team, hired by Daniel Grace, arrived to mow and trim, Jenna nearly turned them away. Mowing was something she and Violet could do. Even Rosemary, who insisted she had a black thumb in regards to anything growing, could trim.

But if she sent them away and the bill Daniel expected didn't arrive, would that pique his interest? If she were him, it would certainly make her wonder. So Jenna let Lennie and his crew perform the duties they'd been hired to do.

After all, when she and Rosemary left, the house would still be here, and the grounds would still require care.

"I'm going to tackle the garden today," Violet announced.

The three of them stood on the back porch, admiring the freshly mowed yard. The garden—or what had once been a garden—must not have been included in the contract for lawn care. Other than removing the weeds creeping between the black iron fencing surrounding the large patch of ground, the crew hadn't touched the garden, which was a tangled mess of grass and weeds.

Rosemary turned to Violet. "Why?"

Violet smiled. "Why what?"

"Why go to all that work? I mean, it's obvious that the owner…" Rosemary paused and corrected herself. "That Daniel isn't interested in the garden."

Since Jenna was supposed to be Daniel's intended, they'd decided they couldn't go around calling him "the owner" without arousing suspicion.

"It doesn't matter whether he's interested or not." Violet studied the area, a thoughtful look on her face. "This house was once a home with a thriving garden. We've brought life back into the house. We need to bring life back to the garden."

"You go, girl." Rosemary fist-bumped with Violet. "Count me in."

"Ah, Rosemary." Jenna cleared her throat. "Remember what happened to the spider plant?"

Rosemary chuckled and waved a dismissive hand. "I have no idea how that plant made the easiest-to-grow list."

"I'd love your help, Rosemary." Violet smiled. "We make a dynamic team."

Jenna opened her mouth, then shut it without speaking. She

couldn't deny that Violet's higher expectations of Rosemary's level of activity had already yielded positive results.

Back in Philadelphia, Jenna had always been inclined to give Rosemary a pass on helping out.

Not here. They each took turns cooking and setting the table when it was time for meals. On Monday, Rosemary had even helped Beverly with the dusting when she'd come to clean.

Though Jenna believed there had been more talking going on than dusting, it had warmed her heart to see her great-aunt so, well, so engaged with another person.

Because of the iffy safety in the area surrounding their neighborhood in Philadelphia, Rosemary had rarely ventured out without Jenna at her side. And with Jenna working so much, Rosemary had become more and more isolated.

Not here. No, not here.

After Monday's cleaning, Rosemary had informed Jenna that she had agreed to be a substitute in Geraldine and Beverly's card group.

Rosemary had looked so pleased and excited that Jenna hadn't the heart to bring up that they likely wouldn't be here when a sub was needed.

"—the sheet music."

Jenna blinked and realized that while her mind was wandering, Rosemary and Violet had continued talking.

"The sheet music?" Jenna kept her tone offhand, but she could see by the humor dancing in Violet's eyes that her inattention had been noticed.

"I opened up the seat of the piano in the first parlor yesterday and found it full to the top with sheet music." Rosemary's expression turned wistful. "When I was a girl, my mother taught me to play. But sheet music was expensive, and money was dear..." Rosemary's voice trailed off.

"Seeing all that sheet music takes you back to those days in

Ludlow." Violet touched Rosemary's arm. "To all those special memories."

"Ludlow?" Jenna asked.

"In Illinois. It's where I lived when we had a piano." Rosemary's smile flashed, then dimmed. "We had to sell the upright when we moved."

Jenna focused on Violet. "How did you know she lived in Ludlow?"

Violet smiled. "It doesn't matter. What matters is that now Rosemary has all the sheet music she could ever want."

While Violet and Rosemary headed to the garden to play in the dirt, Jenna went to the basement.

The washer and dryer were located close to the bottom of the steps. Until today, that was as far as Jenna had gone. She'd had no need to venture farther.

It was clear that this area, like the garden, had been neglected. Obviously, Beverly's contract to clean didn't extend to the lower level.

Stepping deeper into the cavernous area, she used pull chains on single lightbulbs to light her way. Here, cobwebs dangled from rafters, and dust coated surfaces of boxes, furniture and curios.

Though the dust made her want to sneeze and she had never been a fan of underground anything, excitement coursed up her spine. This was something she could do. Her work down here would be her way of giving back, like Violet and Rosemary's work in the garden. Perhaps then she wouldn't feel so guilty about living in this wonderful house without permission.

They'd been here a week, and with each passing day, the house had begun to feel more like not just a home, but *her* home. Something she'd never had.

With her father in the military, they'd moved frequently. Jenna had never let herself get too attached. Shortly before she'd received her license as a registered nurse, her mother had died from an aggressive cancer. Six months later, a massive heart attack had taken her dad.

In recent years, the closest thing to home Jenna had ever had was the apartment she'd shared with Rosemary. Though being with her great-aunt was wonderful, the apartment had never been a home.

How was it that this house could so quickly evoke that sentiment? It was almost as if the place had wrapped its arms around her and said, "Welcome home." As if the house had been waiting for her, knowing she would care for and love it.

Jenna chuckled at the fanciful image, but couldn't shake the feeling of rightness. Pushing all those thoughts aside, she walked deeper into the basement and found even more boxes and furniture.

Surveying the area, Jenna came up with a plan. First, she would get rid of the cobwebs and the dust. She would vacuum and scrub, then organize.

While she didn't want to get ahead of herself, it seemed sensible to have all the boxes stored in the same area of the basement. Since they didn't appear to be sealed, she would check inside—though she would really try not to pry—then label and seal and put them in an orderly fashion.

Once she'd cleaned, she would get some drop cloths and cover the furniture.

Though she had her work cut out for her, Jenna was eager to begin. She wasn't a stranger to hard work, and doing this for the house would be a labor of love.

Hopefully, putting this basement in order would assuage her guilt over staying in a house that wasn't hers and where she had no right to be.

CHAPTER FOUR

The trip to Marco Island hadn't produced the results Daniel had hoped. He wasn't sure if the end result would have been different if he'd been in the spacious home with the amazing view of the gulf by himself. Even though Calista had tried to keep out of his way so he could write, he'd reminded himself this was a mini vacation for her, too.

The realization that he needed to have a heart-to-heart with Calista about their personal relationship was his only takeaway from the trip.

Being involved with her had become...confusing. The lines between editor and girlfriend had gotten blurry. He couldn't tell if she liked him for who he was or because his book made her publishing house money.

He would wait for the right time, and then he would be honest with Calista. First and foremost, she was a smart and savvy businesswoman with a strong desire to get ahead. He knew that working with Daniel Grace, *NYT* bestselling author, was much more important to her than their personal relationship.

The weekend had taught him something else. The next time he needed to get away, he would go alone. He would pick a place where he could be assured of privacy and where he could concentrate.

～

With her hand on the front doorknob, Jenna paused and turned back to her aunt. "Are you sure you don't want to come with us? You love antique stores, and this one has a stellar reputation."

Today, Jenna and Violet would continue their exploration of GraceTown by visiting several businesses located in the town's historic district. The primary one Jenna wanted to scope out was Timeless Treasures. She'd read online about the business and its proprietor, Sophie Wexman.

The woman had a reputation for selling "timeless treasures." Jenna hoped to find a small item that would remain in the house when they left, a token of thanks to Daniel Grace. It couldn't cost much, because Jenna couldn't afford much, but she was hopeful she would find just the right item.

"I appreciate the offer, but I haven't played the piano in years, and I'm itching to sit down and tickle the ivories." Rosemary stood between the colonnade that separated the foyer from the parlor, looking spring-ready in a housedress covered in tiny sprigs of yellow flowers. "Since I'm not sure how good I'll be, I relish the thought of this time alone."

"We won't be long—"

"Don't rush on my account." Rosemary waved an airy hand. "You two girls have fun. Visiting local shops, trying out something we left behind long ago, well, it's all part of our grand adventure."

Jenna hated that she couldn't be honest with her aunt about the reason behind this grand adventure. She was only grateful that Rosemary had embraced this time and was thriving.

"Grand adventure." Once outside, Violet slanted a glance at Jenna. "I can't believe Rosemary still thinks that's all this is."

The foot Jenna had been placing with great certainty hit an uneven piece of sidewalk, pitching her forward.

Feeling herself falling, Jenna fought for balance. She might have hit the sidewalk, but Violet reached out, taking her arm, steadying her until she regained her balance.

A familiar, energizing force rushed through Jenna. She turned toward Violet, oddly breathless. "Thanks for the save."

"That's what I'm here for."

"You know, don't you?" Jenna braced herself, recalling Violet's cryptic comment early on.

Violet shrugged.

"What is it you think you know?" Jenna pressed, no longer content to let the subject drop.

Violet lifted a hand and began counting off on her fingers. "Cash-only road trip. Only giving first names. Not wanting people to see your license plate."

Jenna couldn't stop herself from emitting a sound of distress. She thought she'd done such a good job and had been so careful. But if Violet could see through her, then Rosemary…

"Jenna."

Violet's soothing tone had Jenna refocusing.

"I hope you know that whatever you're hiding from—real or imagined—I've got your back."

Tears sprang to Jenna's eyes. This burden had been a heavy one to carry alone. But was it right to bring Violet fully into it?

"You've been there for me," Violet continued. "Whatever you're running from, you have a good reason."

"I want to tell you all about it." Jenna bit her bottom lip and shifted uneasily from one foot to the other. "But I—"

"I'm here for you, Jenna." Violet met her gaze, the sunlight dancing like a halo on her curls. "You can trust me."

Jenna considered. Hadn't she read somewhere that for a friend, being entrusted with another's burdens was a privilege?

Deciding it was time to take a plunge into the honesty pool,

Jenna gestured to a bench positioned under a leafy oak not far from the walkway. "We'll sit, and I'll tell you."

Once they were seated, Jenna shifted her body toward Violet. "When you were at the group home, I believe I mentioned that my day job was working as a private-duty nurse."

Violet nodded, her fathomless blue eyes never leaving Jenna's face.

"I was the caregiver for the spouse of a city official." Normally, Jenna wouldn't divulge even that much, but there were lots of officials in a city the size of Philadelphia, and the fact that Mr. Menard held such an important position was relevant to the story. "His spouse told him I'd lost my second job. When I finished my shift, he called me into his home office."

Though Violet remained silent, Jenna could see she had the girl's total attention.

Just remembering what had happened next had a lump forming in Jenna's throat. She cleared her throat in an attempt to dislodge it, but it didn't work. Tears stung the backs of her eyes.

"Take your time." Violet's soft voice comforted and soothed. "Here for you. Remember?"

Jenna expelled a shuddering breath and found her center. "He appeared confident that he had a solution to my unexpected loss of income. I thought, I hoped, he knew of a weekend nursing position that was open. Or maybe he was going to offer me a raise."

"It wasn't either of those things, was it?"

The sympathy in Violet's voice was nearly Jenna's undoing. She shook her head fiercely from side to side. Then, she laid it all out, ending with the "job" he'd offered her.

"Sleazeball," Violet muttered.

The word brought a smile to Jenna's lips, a smile that quickly faded as she continued with the story.

"When I refused and turned to leave, he grabbed me. He had

this dark look in his eye when he told me he would show me what I'd be missing. I fought to get free, but he was too strong."

Violet's steady gaze never left her face.

Jenna took a couple of steadying breaths before continuing. "When he momentarily released his grip on my wrist to t-touch me, I knew I had to do something to make him release his hold so I could get away. The paperweight was on the desk and in reach. I grabbed it and hit him with it. He let go, and I ran."

Violet nodded. "You did what you had to do."

"I did. When I got into my car and drove off, I honestly thought that would be the end of it. I would call the agency that had placed me and let them know I wouldn't be back."

"Yet you felt the need to leave town?"

Despite the question, Jenna had the feeling Violet already knew why. But that couldn't be. She'd gotten only to the part of the story where she'd hit Mr. Menard with the paperweight and run out.

"My friend Britta, who works for the family as a housekeeper, called me shortly after I left." Jenna relayed the rest of the story.

"Not only was the city official willing to lie, so was his assistant." Violet spoke slowly.

"That's right." Anger bubbled inside Jenna, but she tamped it down. "To fight the charges, I would have had to rely on a public defender. I could see the sleazeball—perfect word for him, by the way—encouraging the district attorney to go for the maximum sentence."

"If I went to jail, Rosemary would be alone. My aunt has spent her life giving to others. If she was down to her last dollar and someone on the street needed help, she'd give it to them."

Violet's lips curved for the first time since Jenna had begun her story. "Rosemary has a giving spirit."

"Too giving." Jenna expelled a breath. "I worried how she'd survive without me. Which is why I withdrew all the money I had in savings and suggested—"

"A road trip."

"Yes."

"Why haven't you confided in your aunt? You have to know she'd support your actions."

"She would," Jenna agreed, "but Rosemary has heart issues. I was concerned the stress might be too much for her to handle."

"You decided to bear the burden alone. Take it all upon yourself, as you've always done."

Jenna gave a little shrug. "I didn't see I had much choice this time."

"You're not alone, Jenna." Violet's soft tone wrapped around Jenna's heart like an embrace. "You've never been alone."

"I opened up to you, well, because something told me I can trust you."

"You can trust me." Violet wrapped her arms around Jenna and squeezed tight. "Absolutely and completely."

Jenna could have been happy simply standing on the sidewalk and gazing through the front window of Timeless Treasures. "The reviews were right. This antique store is in a class by itself."

Violet reached for the ornate door handle of the shop. "I'm guessing there is even more inside to see."

Laughing, Jenna pulled her gaze away from the display of vintage lunch boxes in the window. "Sorry. Antiques are my weakness."

"Did your parents collect?"

"No, they were into what I'd call modern minimalism." Jenna thought of all the homes they'd lived in, both on military bases and in communities. "My mom told me she never got too attached to any item since it was just one more thing to pack up. She preferred to keep things simple."

"You understood."

"I did, but I love the idea of passing special things down from one generation to the next. Of having something that your grandmother or great-grandfather had, that reminds you of the kind of person they were." Jenna's voice turned dreamy. "I think that's why I'm enjoying living where we are right now. There's so much history in the house. I know this might sound corny, but I can practically feel the love of those who've gone before inside those walls."

"Not corny at all." Violet pulled the door open and stepped to the side. "Let's see if we can find something in here that evokes that same wonderful feeling."

"Welcome to Timeless Treasures." A tall brunette—she had to be at least six feet tall—greeted them as soon as they entered the shop. Then she paused and stared at Violet. "You look familiar. Have you been here before?"

"We're both first-timers." Violet spoke before Jenna could.

"Well, I'm so glad you decided to check us out. I'm Ruby. Sophie, the owner, is the one over there ringing up a sale."

Ruby paused, studying Violet. "Are you certain we haven't met before?"

"Positive."

"Okay, sorry to keep asking. There's just something about your face." Ruby's look said she still wasn't convinced that their paths hadn't crossed.

"It's probably the hair." Violet patted her curls.

Like Violet's own curly 'do, the woman's hair exploded around her pretty face in a riot of curls.

"That might be it." The woman chuckled. "It's always a pleasure to meet another curly girly."

"I'm Violet. And I prefer 'curly fry' to 'curly girly.'"

Ruby waved a long, elegant hand. "Po-tay-to, Po-tah-to."

"This is Jenna." Violet gestured with her head. "My big sister."

"I saw the resemblance the minute you two walked through the door." Ruby grinned. "It's a pleasure to meet you both."

A loud buzz sounded from Ruby's pocket. A look of regret crossed her face. "That's my reminder that I need to get on the road. I'm attending an auction this afternoon that has some prime antiques."

Jenna smiled. "Good luck."

"I'm excited…and hopeful." Ruby's gaze shifted from Jenna to Violet. "If you have any questions, Sophie will be happy to assist you."

Jenna slanted a glance at Violet as they stepped deeper into the store. "She was convinced she's seen you before."

"I have one of those faces." Violet gave a dismissive flick of her wrist, as if bored with the topic. "Where shall we look first?"

As she and Violet explored the store, Jenna inhaled the pleasing scent of orange. There was much to admire in this shop, starting with the way the antiques were displayed.

An antique dining room table had been set up as if a dinner party were imminent. A glittering chandelier hung about three feet over the center of the table, casting prisms of light outward.

China, crystal and silverware were showcased on the table. The crisp linen napkins at each place setting were folded in a style Violet recognized. "That napkin style is called the bishop's hat. It was popular in wealthy households in the 1920s."

Jenna widened her eyes. "How do you know that?"

Violet shrugged. "It's featured in dozens of old movies."

They moved on to an area filled with vintage cleaning equipment and tools, everything from an old Hoover floor scrubber to floor sweepers from the early 1900s.

Mannequins modeling clothing from a variety of decades had them wandering over to check the inventory. So far, Jenna hadn't found anything she wanted to buy to leave behind as a gift.

"I love this. It is so me." Violet held up a bright pink minidress in a paisley pattern. "I must have it."

Jenna thought of her dwindling supply of cash. "How much is it?"

"Don't worry." Violet shot her a sunny smile. "I've got money."

Jenna wasn't sure how, but she didn't argue. "It's super cute."

While Violet perused the rest of the dresses, Jenna approached a display that featured an assortment of books and fountain pens sitting atop a vintage desk.

Jenna's eyes were immediately drawn to the books. There was something here for every taste, from leather-bound college year-books going back to the 1920s to early editions of classic favorites.

An elegant art nouveau book holder from the early 1900s caught her eye and had her stepping closer. For display purposes, the holder held an assortment of envelopes, all addressed with elegant penmanship and boasting interesting stamps.

The brass holder appeared sturdy enough to hold not only mail, but magazines as well. Jenna liked that the small, roughly five-by-five-inch size was big enough to serve a purpose without being too obtrusive.

Leaning over, she lifted the tag. It was more than she wanted to spend, but Jenna reminded herself they were living rent-free.

After carefully removing the envelopes and setting them on the desktop, Jenna picked up the holder.

Violet smiled when she saw what Jenna held. "We each found something."

They made their way to the counter, where the owner was ringing up another sale. Sophie had dark hair, hazel eyes and a smile as friendly as Ruby's. She flashed that smile again as she handed the customer a sack. "Thank you. Please visit us again soon."

Once the man walked away, Sophie turned to them.

"I'm sorry I couldn't greet you before this." Sophie raked a hand through her silky hair and blew out a breath. "It's been crazy today. A good problem to have, but I really like spending time to help customers. Do you have any questions?"

"You have a lovely store." Jenna let her gaze sweep the shop.

"It must be wonderful to own a business that deals in objects that once meant something to someone."

"It is." Sophie's curious gaze shifted from Jenna to Violet.

Jenna watched her eyes linger half a beat longer on Violet before returning to her. She braced herself for the comment about Violet looking familiar.

Instead, Sophie extended her hand. "I'm Sophie Wexman."

"Ruby told us." Violet shifted the dress to her other arm and shook Sophie's hand. "I like her."

Surprise flickered in Sophie's eyes. "You know Ruby?"

"She was leaving when we arrived," Violet explained. "We introduced ourselves, and she told us you were the owner and the one to go to with any questions."

"Which means we know who you are, but you don't know us," Jenna jumped in. "I'm Jenna. This is Violet."

"Jenna and Violet. I've heard about you." Sophie's smile widened. "You're living in the house originally built by Richard F. Grace. Do you know he was one of the first people in Grace-Town to buy a Model T at Huston Ford, which was the earliest car dealership in the area?"

"How do you know all that?" Jenna asked, delighted to add that piece of information to her knowledge of the house.

"I have my sources." Sophie smiled and inclined her head. "Will you and your fiancée be making your home in GraceTown?"

Jenna hesitated. So many ways to answer that question, but all would require further lies.

"So far, what I see I like," Jenna deflected, then acted as if something had caught her eye. "Oh no, I want to check out one more thing before I have you ring up my purchase."

"Go." Violet gave her a little push. "Take your time. We're in no rush."

Jenna pulled out some cash and placed the money and the holder on the counter. She turned to Violet. "Why don't you pay for this book holder and your dress while I check out the glassware?"

"Stellar plan." Violet's eyes held a knowing gleam.

Before Jenna could step away, a small stone angel on the counter, not more than five inches tall, caught her eye. Picking it up, she turned to Sophie. "This is different."

"It's a replica of the stone angel statue in the town square." Sophie smiled. "I always keep a few on hand. Tourists like to buy them as souvenirs."

Jenna turned the angel over in her hand. "Why is there an angel in the town square?"

"Town lore is that a young woman showed up out of nowhere to nurse the sick during the Spanish influenza outbreak in 1918." Sophie appeared to warm to the topic. "She went from house to house, wherever she was needed, without regard for her own health. It's said that once the crisis was over, she disappeared. The community was so grateful, they called her their angel and erected the statue in her honor."

Jenna studied the statue more closely, then shifted her gaze to the girl at her side. "Omigosh, Violet, this angel looks just like you."

"Well, actually," Sophie said before Violet could respond, "it kind of looks like both of you."

Violet smiled. "Of course it does. Because we're sisters."

Jenna laughed and set down the statue. "I'm going to do a quick check of the Depression glassware display."

Sophie didn't say anything more about the angel as she rang up the sales and put the items in separate bags.

Jenna was rejoining them at the counter when Violet reached for the sacks.

Sophie touched Violet's hand and said, "You know, Grace-Town is known for unexplainable happenings."

Violet cocked her head. "You mean, like people traveling through time?"

Jenna felt her eyes widen. Where had that come from?

Sophie didn't look the least bit bemused by the comment. "Is that what you're doing?"

"Nope. I'm different than time." Violet picked up the bags. "Right now, that's all you need to know."

CHAPTER FIVE

"There's an angel statue in the town square that looks like Violet."
Jenna took a lace cookie and dipped it in the cup of hot tea Rosemary had brewed.

Rosemary slanted a glance in the girl's direction, a smile tugging at the corners of her lips. "Is that so?"

Violet rolled her eyes. "If it looks like me, which it doesn't, it also looks like Jenna."

Jenna chuckled. "Good point."

Interest glimmered in Rosemary's blue depths. "What I want to know is, why do they have an angel statue in the town square?"

After grabbing a couple of cookies, Violet pushed to her feet. "I've heard this story before. You tell her, Jenna. I'm going inside to listen to music."

"Is everything okay with Violet?" Two lines of concern formed between Rosemary's brows as the screen door fell shut behind Violet.

"I'm not sure. Maybe I shouldn't have brought up the statue, but I thought it was cool how it looks like her." Jenna quickly relayed the story Sophie had told. "And, I guess, like me. It's cool to resemble someone in the past who everyone revered."

Rosemary took a bite of cookie and chewed thoughtfully. "I can see where Violet might find the whole thing troubling."

"Really?" Jenna didn't bother to hide her confusion. "Why?"

"This angel person was a historical figure. Violet, well, she doesn't have much of a personal history." Rosemary paused. "Does she?"

Jenna thought back to Violet's records at the group home. No parents listed. No relatives either. "No, not from what I read."

Jenna considered telling Rosemary about Violet and Sophie's odd time-travel exchange, but she shrugged it off. Maybe Sophie was a bit eccentric, and Violet, in her usual endearing way, had simply played along.

"Violet told us she once lived in this community, but said she had no family left here. She bounced from place to place with nowhere to really call home. Maybe seeing the statue of this woman made her wonder who out there carries her features, the heart-shaped face, the wide mouth, even those gorgeous gold flecks in her blue eyes." Rosemary's expression softened. "If I were her, not knowing would make me sad."

Jenna's heart twisted. "I never thought…" Shame flooded her. She hadn't even considered that possibility. Even when Violet had mentioned she wasn't keen on going to the town square to see an old statue, Jenna had walked in that direction anyway.

Once there, Violet had gazed at the statue and studied the inscription, which said:

Angel of GraceTown
You blessed us with your loving hands in our hour of need
We will remember you always

When Violet had finally turned away, Jenna swore she hadn't been the only one with tears in her eyes.

Jenna found the thought of a woman risking her own life to help so many people she didn't know incredibly moving. That's what she'd been focused on, not a young girl experiencing confusing feelings.

Jenna abruptly stood. "I need to apologize."

Rosemary placed a hand on Jenna's arm. "Maybe give her time to settle and then take your lead from her. There's nothing worse than someone forcing a talk that only magnifies your pain."

"That is something I definitely don't want to do." Impulsively, Jenna leaned over and brushed a kiss across Rosemary's cheek. "Thanks for the insight."

"Anytime." Rosemary lifted her cup of tea. "That's what we seniors are for."

Forcing herself to ignore the nearly overwhelming impulse to immediately go to Violet and apologize, Jenna went to the kitchen and settled at the table with her laptop. She took a couple of calming breaths, then pulled up the website of *The Philadelphia Inquirer*. Searching for both Michael and Cherise Menard yielded a number of old references, but nothing since Jenna had left Philadelphia.

Wanting to be thorough, she put "Michael Menard" in the Google search field, but got nothing that didn't pertain to his role as a councilman.

Relieved but confused, Jenna sat back. Had Britta been mistaken about what she'd overheard? If a crime had been reported, especially one involving an attack on a city councilman, shouldn't there have been something in the news by now?

Maybe the police had told Mr. Menard that they would need to speak with Jenna before deciding whether to pursue charges. For several seconds, she found comfort in that thought, but she couldn't make herself believe it.

She counted her money, relieved to see how much remained. Not paying for lodging was saving her a lot.

Eventually, they would need to find a safe place to live. Although she would like to stay in a smaller community, a large city seemed the best option for someone who was hiding out.

At least—for now, anyway—they were safe. Jenna closed her eyes, reveling in the gentle breeze from the open window caressing her face.

Hearing footsteps, Jenna opened her eyes and turned.

Violet stood in the doorway. "Am I interrupting?"

"Not at all." Jenna closed the laptop. "I'd love company."

"That's good, because I planned to join you whether you wanted me to or not." Violet shot her a cheeky smile.

Though Violet appeared back to her normal cheery self, Jenna believed an apology was in order. "Hey, about earlier, I'm sorry if I was being weird about the statue."

"Please. Nothing to apologize for." Violet waved a dismissive hand. "I'm not upset you think I look like some cheesy souvenir, even if I'm obviously prettier."

Jenna laughed. "Obviously."

Violet might not think an apology was needed, but there were a couple things Jenna wanted—no, needed—to say. "I shouldn't have forced you to go to the square when you didn't want to. I forget you have a connection to this place. I hope you know if you ever want to talk about that, share more of your past, that I'm here to listen."

"Jenna, if I had a problem looking at that statue, I wouldn't have gone with you. And there's nothing that needs to be told when it comes to me and GraceTown. What we should be talking about is your creep of an ex-boss. What news did you find?"

"How did you know I was checking for news?"

Violet glanced pointedly at the laptop.

Jenna expelled a breath. "I didn't find anything, which I guess is a good thing."

"Didn't I tell you not to worry?"

"Still, I need to figure out a plan." Jenna pushed to her feet and began to pace. "We can't stay here."

"Why not? What's wrong with here?"

Jenna wished she could bottle up Violet's cool confidence and implacable composure. "You mean, other than it not being our house?"

"So what?" Violet lifted one thin shoulder in a slight shrug. "We may not be owners, but we're caretakers. The way I see it, we've got a lot of caring still to do."

When Beverly arrived for cleaning on Monday morning, Jenna had coffee ready. Since she, Rosemary and Violet had moved in, coffee and conversation preceded any cleaning.

Today, Geraldine had come with Beverly. She'd brought her toolbox, prepared to fix the hinges on the squeaky back screen door.

"Is this the bad boy?" Geraldine gestured to the door.

"Yes, but it can wait," Jenna told Geraldine. "Violet baked cranberry scones this morning, and I just brewed a fresh pot of coffee. Sit and enjoy."

Geraldine, dressed in coveralls and a train engineer's striped hat over her pixie haircut, shook her head. "I appreciate the offer, but I promised Jolene Kinicki down the block I'd check out her washer after I finished with the door. Can't do without a washer."

"Ain't that the truth?" Rosemary stepped into the room. "I wanted to say hello to both of you before I leave for the market."

"I thought you'd have coffee and scones with us before you left." Jenna offered Rosemary a hopeful smile. Not only did she love having her aunt around, she knew Beverly looked forward to her and Rosemary's "chats."

"Alas," Rosemary said with a dramatic flair, "Margaret from two doors down—"

"I know Margaret," Beverly interrupted. "Lovely woman and a fierce card player."

"Well, Margaret and I got to talking last night and discovered we were both headed to the market this morning, so we decided to ride together."

"Ideal Grocery is having a huge sale this week," Beverly informed Jenna.

"That's where we're headed." Rosemary shot Jenna a look. "There isn't anything I like more than a sale."

Especially, Jenna thought, when money was tight. Normally, she was the one who did the grocery shopping. While Rosemary could handle the shopping, the walk to and from the store would be too much for her.

"Well, we'll miss you—" Jenna began.

A honking horn had Rosemary offering a swift good-bye.

Geraldine looked up from where she knelt beside the screen door. "I've noticed you haven't used your car much since you got to GraceTown."

"Just saving on gasoline." Jenna offered the woman a bright smile, but Geraldine's gaze remained watchful for several heartbeats.

Then the older woman rose and nodded in satisfaction. "A little WD-40, and it's good as new."

"Thank you, Geraldine." Jenna reached for her wallet. "How much do I owe you?"

"For that?" Geraldine brushed the air with her hand. "Save me a scone, and we'll call it good."

"I'll do better than that." Jenna made a great show of placing two scones on a small plate and setting it aside. "I'll save you two."

Geraldine gave her a thumbs-up, then studied Jenna thoroughly. "I shouldn't be long at the Kinickis. If your car is giving you trouble, I can take a gander at it when I get back."

"It runs fine." Jenna forced a lightness to her tone at odds with the rapid beating of her heart. "We all love to walk. It's an easy way to get more exercise in. Plus, like I said, it saves on gas."

The dubious look in Geraldine's eyes said she wasn't entirely convinced, but she only gave a nod before turning her attention to Beverly. "Don't work too hard."

Beverly offered Geraldine a warm smile. "You're the one who's doing all the work. I'm about to enjoy a scone and coffee."

Geraldine chuckled, and as she stepped out the back door, she shoved a grease rag into one pocket.

Jenna smiled at Beverly. "Looks like it's just you and me today."

"Isn't Violet going to join us?" Beverly asked as she took a seat.

"Not this morning. She's in the garden." Jenna poured two cups of coffee from the carafe on the table. "She likes to get her work done before it gets too warm."

Beverly's lips curved in a soft smile. "She's a lovely girl."

"She is," Jenna agreed.

From the moment she'd met Violet, Jenna had known the young woman was something special. She'd been a bright light at the group home—always willing to listen and lend a helping hand when needed.

Jenna recalled walking into the living room once to find Violet consoling a girl who'd gotten some bad news. "Their loss," she'd heard Violet murmur to the distraught teen. "You're an incredible person."

The girl had sniffled, then flung her arms around Violet.

Even now, simply recalling Violet's kindness to someone she'd barely known, brought a lump to Jenna's throat.

"I always wanted a sister."

Beverly's comment, punctuated by a sigh, pulled Jenna back to the present.

She understood. Like Beverly, she'd longed for a sister, a built-in friend who would make the many difficult moves with her.

At this point in her life, with her parents both gone, a sister would be a connection to her past, as well as a part of her present and future. Confiding in Violet about Mr. Menard had given Jenna a taste of how nice it would be to have someone in her life who'd always have her back and who'd be there for her in good times and bad.

When Jenna realized Beverly expected a response, Jenna smiled. "Violet is pretty nice to have around."

"I imagine she is." Beverly sipped her coffee and studied the scones. "These look yummy."

"Fresh out of the oven this morning," Jenna told her.

Since Rosemary had gone to the market, helping Beverly would fall to Jenna. Though she knew Beverly would protest, there was no way Jenna could stand by and watch the older woman work.

Last week, Rosemary had helped with the dusting, but Jenna would do the floors today, leaving Beverly with the dusting.

Taking a bite of scone, Jenna considered mentioning she was cleaning the basement. The moment the thought surfaced, she shoved it aside. If she did, Beverly would likely offer to help.

"Any word yet on when Daniel will be joining you?" Beverly inclined her head. "You must miss him horribly."

The scone, which had been going down quite nicely, caught in Jenna's throat. It took several seconds for her to regain her composure.

"I'm fine." Jenna cleared her throat and took a long drink of coffee. "What were we talking about again?"

She wiped the tears from the corners of her eyes with a paper napkin.

"Your fiancé. It can't be easy being apart from the one you love for so long." Though Beverly sipped her coffee, her gaze remained riveted on Jenna's face. "I can't imagine being here and having Geraldine in New York."

"Daniel is a great guy." Jenna was determined to stick as close to the truth as possible. From all she'd read, it appeared he was nice. She'd done her research on him once she'd learned he owned this house. She'd not only perused book reviews and press releases, but she'd also read anything she could find on his family and his life growing up.

She'd learned he'd grown up with parents who were active in their community in Connecticut. He had younger siblings, who were now grown with families of their own. He'd never been married and had been a practicing attorney before he took up writing.

Beverly's silence had Jenna adding, "You're right. It's not easy being separated from the one you love."

That, as a general statement, was also true.

"I'm sure he's eager to join you." Beverly appeared determined to push the point. "Any idea when that will be?"

"Everything hinges on how things go with the new book." Jenna broke off another piece of scone and forced a thoughtful expression. "A writer's life is not an easy one."

"Still, you're his fiancée. I can't imagine—"

"A fiancée can be quite a distraction." Jenna added a wink. "If you know what I mean."

Beverly laughed. "I'm sure that's true."

For several minutes, Beverly caught Jenna up on GraceTown happenings. Jenna had begun to feel she knew the people Beverly talked about, even though she'd never met them.

"Charlie just got a new patent approved for another automotive thingy." Beverly waved a hand. "Geraldine could tell you what it is. All I know is that he and Hannah were over the moon. Lisa, too."

"Charlie and Hannah are your neighbors." Jenna took a second to organize the information Beverly had relayed about the couple. "Lisa is Charlie's mother."

"The three of them live together quite happily." Beverly's smile dimmed. "Lisa has MS, and mobility can be an issue."

"It's amazing that it works." At Beverly's curious look, Jenna added, "The three of them living together."

"Lisa understands that Charlie and Hannah are newly married and need their privacy." A soft look filled Beverly's eyes. "Hannah is a lovely young woman, and she adores Lisa, so yes, it works out extremely well."

Jenna wondered what it would be like having Rosemary living with her and her husband when she got married. That was, if she ever did find the right guy and got married. Anyone she fell in love with would have to understand that she and Rosemary were a package deal.

"It's no different, I imagine, than Daniel accepting that your aunt and sister are a part of your life." Beverly sighed at the thought. "That takes a special man."

"Mm-hmm," Jenna murmured, her lips on the rim of her cup.

"I hoped he'd be here when we have our party, but the plans are already in place, and the date can't be changed."

"Party?" Jenna thought she'd been paying attention, but her mind must have wandered at a critical point in the conversation.

"The one Geraldine and I host at the end of April every year. Rosemary said you'd be there." Beverly smiled. "When I mentioned to some of the regular attendees that you and your family are coming, well, let's just say everyone is extremely excited to meet Daniel's fiancée and her family."

CHAPTER SIX

Over dinner that evening, Jenna broached the subject of the party with Violet and Rosemary.

"While I appreciate Beverly and Geraldine inviting us, I'm not sure that attending is wise." Jenna put down her fork to take a sip of tea.

"When Geraldine mentioned the party to me," Rosemary said, "I told her I thought it sounded like fun and, of course, we'd be there." Puzzlement furrowed her brow. "Why would we not go?"

Jenna wasn't about to bring up a possible warrant for her arrest. Rosemary still had no idea what had led to this unexpected road trip. That was just how Jenna wanted to keep it.

She couldn't tell Rosemary she was concerned who might be at that party. The two women were well connected in the Grace-Town community. For all she knew, Beverly and Geraldine might have friends in the police department.

Since Rosemary was aware that they were staying in this house without the owner's permission, Jenna decided to use that as the reason.

"We're living here under false pretenses," Jenna gently reminded her aunt.

"Pishposh." Rosemary waved an airy hand. "We're house-sitting. Let's not make it more than that."

Jenna was all for not making it more than that. She just wasn't convinced the owner of the house or law enforcement would see it that way. Plus, there was the small fact that she was pretending to be Daniel's fiancée. There was no way she'd be able to defer all the questions about their relationship at a party.

Rosemary's expression turned pleading, as if she sensed Jenna wasn't convinced. "Please, Jenna. It's been so nice being part of a community. I haven't had that since I was your age."

Violet, who'd risen to grab the pepper, paused by Jenna's chair and placed a hand on her shoulder. "I recall you telling me how isolated Rosemary—and you—were in Philadelphia. This party is another step toward a satisfying and happy life for both of you."

The girl wasn't speaking about her needs, Jenna knew, but her aunt's. Rosemary had begun to blossom in this community.

Jenna reminded herself that her online searches for news about Mr. Menard's "assault" had turned up nothing so far. Why was she so worried about Daniel Grace, who was in New York City, likely focused on writing his next novel?

"You know, I can't recall the last time I went to a party."

Rosemary's blue eyes flashed brightly. "Are you saying you think we should go?"

Jenna glanced at Violet for a second and received a slight nod before returning her attention to Rosemary. "Let's do it."

When Calista texted Daniel and asked if he could drop by her office later that morning, he didn't hesitate. He hoped a few hours away from the blank computer screen would jump-start his creativity and help him decide where to start the next scene.

An hour later, Daniel sat with Calista in her office in Midtown Manhattan. For several minutes, they spoke about everything except his work in progress. She brought up similar books that would be releasing from other publishers and what marketing would be doing to set his apart.

Daniel opened his mouth, ready to come clean about his struggles and his fear about finishing this book, when she spoke first.

"Daniel, I need you to be straight with me. You know I've done all I can to get you extensions. But we've got lots of marketing dollars sunk into this book and a publicity window that won't last forever." Calista's gaze searched his face. "I want you to be successful, but I can't help you if you're not honest with me. Tell me what's going on."

He hesitated for a long moment. Over the past month, each time she'd asked, he'd given her the impression the book was coming together. Obviously, she had become adept at reading between the lines.

"What's going on is I'm struggling. Maybe my dad was right, and I should have stuck with the law. At least I was good at that." Frustrated and embarrassed, Daniel pushed to his feet and began to pace. "I don't know what's wrong with me. When I look at what I've written, I shudder. It's the trifecta—stale, unimaginative and trite."

Instead of telling him she was sure it was wonderful or some other equally inane comment, she grew thoughtful, and when she finally spoke, her words were measured.

"I know I've said this before, but what you're experiencing happens frequently with a second book, even without the pressure of having the first be a monster hit." Her tone remained light, but he saw understanding in her blue depths. "We can work together on what you've got to make it great. You're a fabulous storyteller, Daniel. The scenes that you come up with are unique and amazing. Not to mention you have a voice and a style that readers love."

Daniel continued to pace. That all might be true about the

first book, but this one was different. Still, he appreciated the compliment. "Thank you for that."

"I loved working with you on the first book, and I know this one will have the same magic."

Her faith in him should have eased his worry, but the fear and frustration went too deep. "I keep thinking maybe I only had one good book in me."

"I don't believe that, and neither do you." The look in her eyes projected confidence in this project and in his ability.

Calista was a straight shooter, someone who never shied away from the difficult. The last thing Daniel wanted to do was disappoint her. He liked Calista, admired her work ethic and her talent.

Six months ago, they'd started dating. Three months ago, he'd moved in with her when his lease ran out. Though his admiration for her hadn't waned, their personal relationship hadn't developed as either of them had hoped. Instead of growing closer as time went on, they'd grown further apart.

But right now, he had more important things on his mind, like an unfinished manuscript.

"Daniel, I'm not sure this is the time." For the first time since he'd stepped into her office, Calista appeared unsure. "I'm not sure there is a good time."

"What is it?"

"You're a great guy, but mixing a personal relationship with business isn't working for me. I've given this a lot of thought, and I believe it's best if we go back to a purely professional relationship."

Though her expression remained placid and her tone matter-of-fact, he saw the regret in her eyes.

"Which," she added, "means I obviously don't think we should continue living together."

And the hits, Daniel thought, *just keep coming.*

Though he'd seen their relationship headed in this direction, he hadn't seen it occurring during this meeting.

"I'm sorry." Worry furrowed her brow. "I've had the feeling that this is what you want, too, or I'd have found a different way and time to bring it up."

Quickly regrouping, he offered a smile. "Clear and concise messaging. No rewriting or editorial input needed. And you're right, it's not unexpected."

"We could talk about it if you want…"

"I don't think there's anything to discuss." Daniel dropped back into the seat he'd vacated only minutes before. "I'm good with returning to the relationship we had before we started dating."

Calista gave a slow nod.

"I won't be going to the UK with you." As Daniel had yet to purchase a ticket, and since the trip was only a week away, she likely hadn't expected him to go anyway.

Calista planned to be gone for three weeks, first to attend a writers' conference, then to meet up with other publishers and authors. At Christmas, they had discussed him going along, but that had been when they'd both thought the book would be done.

"I assumed you'd want to stay and use that time to write and find a place to live."

Daniel grinned. "Go ahead, crack the whip and tell me I better have some pages for you by the time you return."

"I'd love some pages." Calista returned his smile, then her tone turned businesslike. "We don't have a lot of time, but we have some. I believe once you take the pressure off yourself to produce, the words will flow."

They were back on familiar ground, a fact Daniel appreciated.

"The pressure is definitely an issue." Daniel gave a little laugh, though he didn't find anything humorous in the situation. "The first book came so easily."

"The process of how each book evolves is unique. The differences between one book and the next can be huge." Her eyes were serious now. "Sometimes, the words come fast and furious. Other times, the story needs to percolate. I firmly believe that once it all comes together in your head, the words will flow, and the story will make it onto the page."

"I keep hoping for that to happen, but so far…"

"Now, this is just a suggestion—it may work for you, and it may not."

"Lay it on me."

Calista's red lips quirked up. "I've had other writers tell me that when they feel stuck, sometimes a change of scenery helps."

"Are you saying you think I should go to London with you after all?"

Her look of startled surprise had him laughing out loud.

"Just kidding."

"I was actually thinking more of you taking your laptop to a coffeeshop or park." Reaching over, she placed a hand on his arm. "Regardless of where it's written, this book is going to be fabulous. I just know it."

On Friday night, Jenna stood beside a large jade plant in Beverly and Geraldine's living room, sipping a watermelon martini and taking a few quiet moments to steady herself. The party, which she'd envisioned as a neighborhood get-together, had ended up being so much more.

Tables of food had been set up inside and outside. There was a wide variety of drinks available, including an assortment of specialty cocktails.

When they'd first arrived, Beverly had taken it upon herself to introduce Jenna, Rosemary and Violet to as many people as possible. Then she'd stepped aside to let them mingle.

For over an hour, that's what Jenna had been doing, while dodging questions about Daniel and her own background. She'd always considered herself to be an open book. The incident with Mr. Menard had put an end to that. She couldn't risk saying something that might eventually bring the police to her door.

Which meant she couldn't let herself fully relax the way she'd have liked.

For a second, Jenna considered asking Rosemary if they could cut this short. But when she spotted her great-aunt chattering animatedly with widower Barry Whitehead, a man Jenna had discovered lived down the block and around the corner from them, she couldn't bring herself to interrupt.

Seeing Rosemary so happy turned Jenna's insides to mush. She could hardly believe how, in such a short span of time, Rosemary had developed a circle of friends. Not simply casual acquaintants, but good friends like Geraldine, Beverly and Margaret. Every day, her aunt expanded the circle.

Recalling how isolated Rosemary had been in Philadelphia brought a flood of guilt. Whatever she had to do, Jenna vowed that their next residence would be in a safe area, one where Rosemary wouldn't have to be afraid to take walks on her own. One where she could make friends and enjoy life to the fullest, like she was doing in GraceTown.

Even if Jenna had to work three jobs, she vowed to make that happen.

"What's up?" Violet popped what looked like a potato chip covered in some sort of dense seasoning into her mouth.

"What is that you're eating?" The chips gave off a slight seafood scent.

Violet licked the residue off her lips. "Crab chips. Beverly said it's the Chesapeake Bay crab seasoning that makes them so yummy."

While Jenna watched, Violet grabbed another chip.

Jenna smiled. It was good to see Violet so passionate, even if it was about potato chips. "I'm definitely going to have to give them a try."

"They're in this humongous bowl in the other room." Violet gestured with one hand, then cocked her head and studied Jenna. "Now what's up with you?"

Jenna lifted her martini glass. "I'm simply enjoying this amazing martini and thinking how happy Rosemary looks."

"She and Barry appear to have hit it off." Violet's lips quirked upward. "Do you know they were both at Woodstock?"

"You're making that up."

"Scout's honor." Violet tried to form her fingers into the Girl Scout salute, but gave up and laughed. "Okay, so I was never a Girl Scout, but they were both at Woodstock."

"I believe you." Jenna couldn't recall a time when the girl had lied to her.

Violet laughed again. "Well, that's a relief."

Jenna liked the sound of Violet's laughter. It appeared that of the three of them, Jenna was the only one on edge this evening. "What have you been up to this evening? Other than enjoying the crab chips."

"First, tell me what put that fierce look on your face when I walked up."

Jenna made a dismissive sound. "I don't do fierce."

"Oh, you most certainly do." Violet softened the comment with a cheeky smile. "Now, spill."

Jenna had the feeling Violet wouldn't give up until she got the information she was after. Even after glancing around to make sure no one was within earshot, Jenna still lowered her voice.

"I am determined that when we leave here, I'm going to make sure our next stop is somewhere Rosemary can feel safe and where she can," Jenna hesitated, knowing what she was about to say would sound corny as heck, but it was the truth, "blossom."

Violet didn't laugh or even crack a smile. "What about you?"

"I can blossom anywhere."

"Not true." Violet shook her head. "You weren't blossoming in Philadelphia."

Jenna hesitated. "You're probably right."

"I am right." Violet spoke in a matter-of-fact tone. "Know what else I'm right about?"

"Noooo," Jenna drew out the word, "but I have a feeling you're going to tell me."

"This is a fun party with lots of interesting people." Violet gestured to the crowd with her head. "I saw you mingling earlier. Now, you're not. Why is that?"

Jenna struggled to put into words the confusing feelings. "I started to feel as if I was playing a part, not being authentic, if you know what I mean. I don't like that feeling."

"It's not an either/or thing. Maybe if you keep the conversation focused on the town or on the party or really on anything other than Daniel Grace and your past, you can let them get to know the real Jenna. The one Rosemary and I love and admire."

Violet's eyes pinned her, and Jenna felt the punch.

"Get out of this corner and have fun." Violet's gaze, serious and steady, made it clear that arguing would be futile.

"You don't have to pound it into me. I get it." Still, Jenna made no move to rejoin the festivities.

"Obviously not." Violet gave her a not-so-soft shove toward the guests. "Go. Fun."

Jenna considered Violet's advice as she stepped forward. So much of tonight's conversation had been focused on her and Daniel.

That in itself made her uncomfortable. She'd always been better at finding out about other people's lives rather than talking about her own. Perhaps Violet was right. What she needed to do was to focus on others. Get to know them and what mattered to them.

Perhaps learn more about GraceTown in the process.

With renewed energy and determination, Jenna set out to enjoy the party.

CHAPTER SEVEN

Over the next hour, Jenna spoke with so many new people her head swam. Her plan, to keep the conversation focused on anything other than her and Daniel Grace, had worked remarkably well.

She found herself actually enjoying the evening.

She'd been having a conversation with Dwight Richards, a neighbor of Beverly and Geraldine's who'd entertained party-goers earlier in the evening on the guitar while his son, Eli, had sung and played the keyboard.

From him, she'd learned that, now that the weather was cooperating, she could expect parties and community events every weekend.

Somehow, she'd managed to keep a smile on her face and respond as if that was a good thing.

When Dwight excused himself, Jenna spotted Sophie by the table of appetizers, as opposed to the table of main dishes and the very popular dessert table. With so much food, it only made sense to categorize the tables.

Jenna approached Sophie and touched the woman's arm. "It's nice to see you again."

Sophie turned, and her face lit up. "Jenna. I saw you when Joe and I first arrived, and I've been hoping for a chance to chat, but every time I looked in your direction, you were surrounded."

"When Beverly said she was hosting a party, I never expected so many people." Jenna glanced at the man with wavy blond hair that brushed his collar who stood beside Sophie.

"Jenna, this is my husband, Joe Wexman." Warmth filled Sophie's voice. "I told Joe all about meeting you and your sister at the shop."

"It's a pleasure to meet you, Jenna." Joe's brown eyes shone with good humor. "When Sophie told me that you're marrying Daniel Grace, I was excited. I'm descended from the Huston family. Josiah Huston knew Richard Frederick Grace, your fiancé's great-great-great-grandfather."

"Sophie mentioned that he was one of the first to buy a Ford from your family's auto dealership." Jenna, whose parents had never shown an interest in family lineage, was fascinated by the idea of someone having all this information about their ancestors. "You must be interested in genealogy."

"It kind of goes with the territory."

At Jenna's puzzled glance, Joe continued. "I'm a professor of folklore and mythology studies at Collister College."

"That's fascinating." Jenna hadn't even known such studies existed. "What's involved in a folklore curriculum?"

"The program focuses on folklore and mythology in a variety of cultures. We look at how a group or society defines itself by looking at everything from its music and folktales to its customs and laws."

Jenna sipped her martini and, for the next fifteen minutes, found herself drawn into a discussion of the topic.

"I told Joe he couldn't have come to a better place than Collister College to teach this topic and oversee the program." Sophie placed a hand on her husband's arm.

When the two exchanged smiles, Jenna felt as if she was

missing a critical puzzle piece that everyone but her possessed. "Why is that?"

"Because GraceTown is known for its unexplainable happenings," Sophie said.

"I heard something about that, but I don't understand exactly what kinds of unexplainable happenings we're talking about." Jenna shifted her gaze from Sophie to Joe. "Nobody has given me any examples."

"Like, ah, people talking to family members who have passed away," Sophie offered.

"Or experiencing time travel," Joe added.

He carefully avoided looking at his wife, which had Jenna wondering if this was one "happening" that Sophie found particularly hard to swallow.

It struck Jenna that this was the second time someone had brought up time travel. She could see Joe being open to at least the possibility, considering the kinds of folktales that were part of his area of study.

Jenna took a thoughtful sip of her drink and carefully considered her words, not wanting to offend. "The seeing and talking to the dead I can accept. I've cared for a number of patients near death who report seeing relatives and friends who've already passed. But time travel…"

Once again, Joe exchanged a glance with his wife.

Jenna shook her head. "That's a hard one for me to wrap my head around."

"I hear ya." Sophie's smile was warm and filled with understanding. "Took me a while, too."

Enjoying the conversation and about to ask Sophie what had finally changed her mind, Jenna was startled when Violet touched her arm. "I'm sorry to interrupt, but Rosemary says Margaret is ready to leave."

Violet turned to Sophie. "Hello again."

"Hi, Violet." Sophie said to her husband, "Joe, this is the young woman I was telling you about who came into the shop the other day."

"I remember." Interest sparked in Joe's eyes. "I've heard a lot about you."

Jenna wondered what there had been to say. She and Violet hadn't been in Timeless Treasures all that long. Then again, Violet seemed to make an impression on everyone she met.

"All good, I hope." Violet's blue eyes danced with good humor.

"All good," Joe agreed.

Violet flashed a smile, then shifted to face Jenna. "Rosemary is saying good-bye to Lisa Rogan, and Margaret is pulling the car around."

Beverly and Geraldine's neighbors Hannah, Charlie and his mother, Lisa, had been among the first people they'd been introduced to when they'd arrived. Jenna would have liked to have had more time to speak with them, but Beverly had been on a mission to introduce them to as many people as possible before things got busy.

Jenna had wanted to ask Hannah more about her cupcake business, but their paths hadn't crossed again.

"I'm ready." Rosemary appeared, offering a smile to Sophie and Joe before looking at Jenna. "Margaret was starting to feel tired and, believe it or not, so was I."

When Margaret had suggested they all ride together to the party, Jenna had breathed a sigh of relief that she wouldn't have to take her car out and leave it parked at the curb.

The ride home went quickly. Violet raved about all things crab, including those delectable chips, the whole way. Jenna wished she'd taken the time to at least sample one.

After Margaret pulled into the driveway, Jenna waited for Rosemary to exit the passenger side before leaning in the door to say, "Margaret, I really appreciate you giving us a ride to and from the party." She smiled at the older woman with snow-white hair. "I'd love to give you gas money—"

"We're neighbors and friends." Margaret shook her head. "It was my pleasure. I enjoyed the company on the drive."

"Well, thank you." Jenna shut the door and gave a little wave as Margaret backed out of the driveway.

Only when Jenna turned toward the house did she see it. Lights that they'd been so careful to turn off were blazing brightly. Not only on the main level, but upstairs as well.

Jenna's heart slammed against her rib cage. She placed a hand on her aunt's arm. "The lights are on."

Rosemary stared at the house, a tiny frown furrowing the area between her brows. "I swear we turned them off."

"We did turn them off," Violet confirmed.

Unlike Rosemary, who appeared puzzled, Violet appeared unconcerned.

"Someone is in the house." Even as she said the words, Jenna hurried toward the porch and took the steps two at a time.

Her heart continued its erratic rhythm as she pulled the key from her bag. Could Daniel have come home? Knowing he was in NYC finishing his latest novel had her pushing that idea from her mind and latching onto another possibility.

The police? No, if it had been the police, there would have been squad cars with lights flashing on the quiet street.

Unless, somehow, Mr. Menard had found her. Or he'd sent someone.

Jenna told herself not to show fear. Men like Michael Menard thrived on intimidation.

"Maybe we should call the police," Rosemary suggested.

"No!" Jenna and Violet snapped out the word at the same time.

At Rosemary's startled look, Violet placed a hand on the older woman's arm. "Let's all be chill. I'm confident there is nothing to worry about."

Jenna wished she could be so confident.

"Violet, I want you to wait with Rosemary out here."

Rosemary shook her head. "I'm not letting you go in there alone."

"Are you sure you don't want me to come with?" Violet asked in the same tone she might use to ask if Jenna wanted mustard on her hot dog.

"I've got this. You both stay here." Jenna's tone brooked no argument. "I'm going to check things out. I'll leave the front door open. If I scream, Violet, get Rosemary away from the house and call the police. Understand?"

Violet nodded.

"I don't understand why we don't call the police now." Rosemary wrapped fingers that trembled around Jenna's arm. "I don't want you to get hurt."

"I won't get hurt," Jenna said with more confidence than she felt, recalling when she'd tangled with Mr. Menard.

She reminded herself that she'd been unprepared then.

As she stepped into the house, she grabbed an umbrella from the stand.

This time, she was ready.

With Calista due back from the UK in a week, Daniel had put most of his stuff in storage. He'd left New York City with his laptop, one duffel and an uncertain itinerary.

He'd considered driving up to Mohonk. The mountain resort was only ninety miles outside the city, and he'd stayed there before. The incredible views of the surrounding forest might be conducive to writing.

Somehow, instead of turning north out of the city, he chose a different route. It took him a while to realize he was headed toward GraceTown. Since it was over five hours away, he decided he'd have plenty of opportunities to turn in a different direction.

When his aching head made considering any alternative

destinations difficult, he stayed the course. He figured that if the people he paid every month to keep up the house were doing their job, it would be ready for him.

The longer he drove, stopping only at a convenience store to buy a bottle of water and wash down a couple of ibuprofens, the more he realized he didn't care what shape the house was in. All he wanted was to collapse on a bed and burrow under the covers.

Finally, just when he thought he couldn't drive another mile, the house came into sight. Nostalgia washed over him as happy memories flooded through him. At that moment, he couldn't recall why he'd stayed away for so long.

Instead of continuing to the carriage house in the back, he parked the car out front on the street. He sat there for several minutes as wave after wave of nausea washed over him. Every muscle in his body ached, and getting out of the car took what little energy he had left.

With great effort, Daniel slung the messenger bag containing his laptop over his shoulder. He left his duffel in the trunk. Right now, he didn't have the strength to carry both.

He felt himself swaying as he covered the seemingly endless distance to the house.

Sweat dampened his skin, and his headache, well, he really should have taken more than two ibuprofen. The pounding hadn't diminished. Instead, it felt as if an elf were inside his brain, stabbing it with a pickax.

He climbed the steps, keeping a tight grip on the rail in order to not fall.

Once inside, he spotted jackets hanging on the coat tree just inside the front door, as well as a pink umbrella with white polka dots in the umbrella stand. His only goal was to make it to his bedroom.

Later, much later, he'd figure out why this odd stuff was in his house.

Or maybe there was no odd stuff. Maybe there were no coats

or pink umbrellas. Maybe this was simply a hallucination brought on by a fever.

A fever that even now had his body shivering uncontrollably.

After dropping his bag on the sofa, Daniel focused on negotiating the stairs to the second floor with the determination of a wide receiver with the goalposts in sight.

He managed to pull himself up first one step, then another. Every few steps, he stopped, his fingers digging into the railing as the world spun around him.

Once the spinning stopped, he'd start again.

He was on the second floor and on his way to the bedroom when nausea hit him with the force of a tsunami making landfall. His stomach churned. Bile rose in his throat.

Shoving the bathroom door open, he stumbled to the stool and dropped to his knees just in time to be violently sick.

CHAPTER EIGHT

When Jenna reached the bathroom and saw the intruder with his hands braced on both sides of the toilet bowl, his hair and face damp with perspiration, she shifted immediately into nurse mode.

Dropping the umbrella—she doubted this man had the energy to fight off a marshmallow—Jenna grabbed a washcloth and ran it under cool water.

After wringing out the cloth, Jenna crouched beside him. He looked at her with eyes dull with fever. "Who are you? Are you the caretaker?"

Though Daniel Grace didn't look anything like his publicity photos at the moment, Jenna recognized him. She offered a reassuring smile as she wiped his face with the cool cloth. "I'm a nurse. I'm here to help."

He closed his eyes at the gentle ministrations. "A caretaker who's also a nurse. Who has a job like that?"

Jenna only smiled.

"I want to go to bed, but I don't have the strength to make it there." His voice held a raspy edge, as if he hadn't used it for a long time. "Oh no."

He turned his face to the bowl and was sick again.

"Sorry," he murmured, trying to reach up to flush.

Jenna's fingers got there first, and the bowl emptied.

"Nothing to be sorry about." She kept her tone matter-of-fact. During her years as a nurse, Jenna had learned that no matter how grossed out she was by anything she saw or smelled, she never let it show. The sick person was embarrassed enough.

Vomit—well, compared to other things—barely qualified as gross.

"Why don't you stay right where you are for a few minutes to make sure your stomach is settled?" Jenna pulled to her feet. "I'm going to get your bed ready. Okay?"

He gave a nod, then winced.

"Your head hurts?"

"Yes." He cleared his throat. "I took something hours ago."

Jenna nodded, glad that the last time they'd been to the market they'd purchased a few household necessities, like ibuprofen, Tylenol and a thermometer. "Don't move. I'll be right back."

Rosemary and Violet must be frantic with worry, so after casting one last look at Daniel, Jenna hurried down the stairs to the front door.

"Everything is fine." She spoke quickly, not wanting to leave Daniel alone for any longer than necessary. "Come on in."

"What took so long?" Worry etched deep lines in Rosemary's face. "I was about to call the police."

For the first time, Jenna noticed the phone in Rosemary's hand.

Jenna inhaled sharply. "You didn't call, though, did you?"

"I told her you were okay," Violet advised.

"She wouldn't let me call." Rosemary's tone reflected her frustration. "I said someone could be killing you while we stood out here like two lumps of coal."

Regret surged. Jenna placed a hand on her aunt's arm. "I'm sorry."

"Why were the lights on?" Stepping inside, Rosemary glanced around. "What did you find out?"

"Daniel Grace is here."

"What?!" Rosemary's eyes widened, and her mouth formed a perfect O.

"He's sick. Throwing up and feverish." Jenna headed for the stairs. She stopped at the base and turned back. "I'm going to get him into bed. It's best if the two of you stay down here until I've got him settled."

Violet nodded approvingly. "Putting those nursing and people skills of yours to good use."

Unlike Rosemary, Violet acted as if Daniel's arrival was to be expected.

Puzzled, Jenna inclined her head. "You don't seem surprised he's here."

"Very little surprises me." Violet's gaze drifted up the steps. "I believe he's on his feet now."

The conviction in Violet's tone had Jenna sprinting up the stairs. Daniel shouldn't be walking without assistance. Not unless he wanted to fall flat on his face.

In the shape he was in, she couldn't even believe he'd made it to the second floor.

When Jenna returned to the bathroom, she discovered Violet was right.

Daniel stood with his hands now braced on either side of the pedestal sink. He turned his head, and Jenna got her first good look at him.

His handsome face was all lines and planes. In her estimation, he was too thin. His hair, damp with sweat, was a nondescript brown, but his eyes, ah, his eyes were simply magnificent. They were a vivid green that would normally cause anyone to take a second look, though they were dulled with fever now.

"I washed my hands and used the cup."

For a second, Jenna didn't follow, then she realized he was telling her he'd rinsed out his mouth.

"Good." Jenna quickly moved to his side. Just because he was standing now didn't mean he couldn't crumple at any moment. "I'll steady you as we walk slowly to the bedroom."

He studied her with eyes that didn't completely focus. "Who are you again?"

The question came out a raspy croak, telling her that his throat—though he'd not yet complained—was likely sore.

"A nurse." Jenna offered a reassuring smile. "I've been taking care of the house, and now I'm going to take good care of you."

"I need to lie down." Daniel turned a little too quickly and stumbled.

Jenna gripped his arm.

"Slow and steady," she reminded him. "Remember?"

His lips quirked upward. "Yes, ma'am."

It was amazing, Jenna thought, how the man could possess so much charisma in such circumstances.

She and Daniel reached the bed without incident. "Do you feel strong enough to stand alone for a few seconds?"

He hesitated for a long moment. "I think so."

Jenna released her hold on him, watching him closely for any signs of unsteadiness. When she felt confident he wouldn't fall, she quickly turned down the bedcovers, then helped him lower himself to a sitting position.

"I want to lie down."

"Not yet." Crouching in front of him, Jenna unlaced his shoes, then slipped them off. She wouldn't worry about undressing him. That would take some effort, and from his pallor, the short walk to the bedroom had wiped him out.

"Let me help you lie back." After assisting him in swinging his legs up on the bed, Jenna pulled the sheet and light quilt over him.

"I'm cold." His teeth began to chatter.

"I'll get you another blanket."

"Don't go," he said, but by the time the words formed, she was back, spreading not one, but two cotton blankets over him.

"Is this better?" she asked, her gaze searching his face.

"My head is pounding." Daniel brought a hand to his disheveled hair. "Don't leave me."

The plaintive plea touched her heart. Jenna had a feeling that this was a man who normally toughed his way through any illness or injury that came his way. But this one had slammed into him with the force of a freight train.

"I'm here to care for you, remember?" Jenna stroked his hair with a gentle touch. "If I leave, it will be only for a minute and only to get something you need."

"Good." He stared at her for one heartbeat, then another before collapsing against the pillow. His eyes closed, and he exhaled heavily. "That's good."

"Don't worry about anything," Jenna promised in a soft voice. "I'm not going anywhere."

Once Daniel appeared to be resting comfortably, Jenna slipped downstairs to grab a thermometer, ibuprofen and a pitcher of water.

She found Violet and Rosemary waiting for her in the living room. When they turned from where they were seated on the sofa, she saw the questions in their eyes. "Daniel is resting. He's pretty sick. Some sort of stomach bug. I'm going to grab a few things, then head back to his room."

"Poor man." Rosemary made a clucking sound with her tongue.

"Poor us." Jenna's lips quirked up in a wry smile. "Him showing up this way is a disaster."

"Perhaps." Violet shrugged. "Or maybe it's all part of a bigger plan."

"Like God's plan?" Jenna shook her head. "I don't think so."

Violet smiled. "Either way, he's here now, and things are about to get interesting."

~

The next time Daniel opened his eyes, he saw light streaming through the window.

"You're awake." The nurse smiled. "Are you feeling better?"

"Not really." Daniel croaked out the words. His head hurt, and his brain seemed stuck in energy-conservation mode, processing at the pace of a slug.

"You'll feel better if we get you out of those clothes and into something more comfortable."

What she meant to do didn't register until she asked him if he thought he could sit up. "I found some pajamas, likely belonging to your grandfather. They're very soft."

"No." His hand flailed in the air like a flyswatter gone berserk. "I'm fine."

Every muscle and every joint ached. He didn't need to sit up or change clothes. He simply needed to rest.

As if he hadn't spoken, she helped him to a sitting position. Daniel was too weak to resist. He noticed there was a basin of water at the bedside and some towels and washcloths.

"You've been perspiring a lot. I'm going to help you take off this shirt and clean you up a bit." Her tone, coolly competent, was matter-of-fact. "There's nothing like a sponge bath when you're sick."

Any other time, he might have been embarrassed, but he was too sick to care, and she, well, she was a nurse. He could tell by her sure movements and no-nonsense manner that caring for the sick was something she did and did well.

That first day after he arrived went by in a blur. Daniel remembered her cooling his skin with the washcloth, the soft feel of the pajamas and the delicious chicken soup she spooned into his mouth that evening. She propped him up with pillows, her arm around him for support.

"Thank you," Daniel murmured when he finished the soup and his head was back on the pillow again.

"You're very welcome." She pulled the quilt up and tucked it around him, her brown eyes calm and reassuring. "You're doing great. Now, rest awhile."

When she pulled the door closed behind her, Daniel didn't ask whether she was coming back.

He knew he could count on her.

The following morning, Jenna sat across the table from Rosemary and Violet and massaged her temples with two fingers. She heaved a sigh. "I don't even know what day this is. My days are all screwed up."

"Today is Sunday." Rosemary rose, went to the counter and grabbed the coffeepot. Returning to the table, she refilled Jenna's cup first. "I believe you need this more than the rest of us. Did you get any sleep at all last night?"

"A little." Jenna took a long drink of coffee.

"She slept in the chair in his room," Violet informed Rosemary.

"Oh, hon, no wonder you look so exhausted."

"I was worried about him," Jenna admitted, recalling the many times during the night she'd risen to check on Daniel. His fever had had him sweating profusely one minute, then shaking with chills the next. "I wasn't sure that if I went into my room to sleep I'd hear him if he called out for me."

"I'd say something about you needing your rest, too," Rosemary's fork hovered in front of her mouth, "but I know you wouldn't listen."

"I picked some peppermint," Violet told her. "I'll get some tea together for you to take up to Daniel. It's known to help reduce fever."

Jenna inclined her head. As far as she knew, no one had left the house since Daniel had arrived. "Where did you get peppermint?"

"Fresh from the garden." Violet forked off another bite of French toast.

"*Our* garden?" Jenna asked, before remembering the weed patch didn't technically belong to them.

Violet smiled. "Yep. We've got a nice big patch of it, so if you need more, let me know."

"I will. Thank you."

"Tomorrow, I plan to make a broth from wild garlic, ginger-root and rosemary." Violet smiled. "That should have Mr. Daniel Grace feeling like himself in no time."

That's exactly what worried Jenna. So far, Daniel had been too sick to ask many questions. But once he started feeling better, she had no doubt the interrogation would begin.

Last night, while Daniel had slept, she'd searched again for news related to Michael Menard.

The only article she'd found was one speculating that the city councilmember might be planning a run for mayor. Nothing about stolen jewels. Or about her.

For now, things appeared calm on that front, but Jenna knew that could change at any moment.

"Beverly is going to be thrilled to learn Daniel is here." An excited trill ran through Rosemary's words.

"Beverly?" Jenna straightened in her seat and focused on her aunt. "Are you thinking of calling her?"

If Rosemary was, Jenna would squash that plan like a bug.

"No need." Rosemary gave a little laugh. "She'll be here tomorrow to clean. Remember?"

Actually, since arriving home from the party on Friday night to find Daniel tossing his cookies in the upstairs bathroom, Jenna had been on autopilot.

"Like I said, I've lost track of the days." Jenna kept her tone offhand. "I'm going to call Beverly and tell her that you've been under the weather since the party, so it's best she doesn't swing by tomorrow."

"But I feel fine," Rosemary protested.

"She knows that." Violet spread jam on a slice of toast. "Jenna doesn't want anyone stopping over until we get things squared away with Daniel."

"Ohh, now I understand." Rosemary's blue eyes shone with excitement. "I play at being sick so that Beverly doesn't come over."

Jenna realized she'd been wrong to worry that Rosemary might balk at playing along. Her aunt loved to play games, and to her, that's what this was.

"Should I splash some water on my face so it looks like I'm perspiring with fever?" Pushing back her chair, Rosemary eyed the sink.

"Ah, not necessary. You don't need to play sick. I'll tell Beverly. You and Violet will stay close to the house until Daniel feels better and I have a chance to speak with him."

"Splashing water on your face was a good thought, though." Violet gave Rosemary a thumbs-up.

Rosemary beamed. "I'm all about doing my share."

"Great." Jenna smiled. "For now, we all need to stay close to the house."

Violet and Rosemary exchanged looks and nodded.

"I pulled Daniel's car into the carriage house the night he

arrived. He left the keys in it so I didn't have to hotwire it." Violet met Jenna's gaze. "No need having it sit out."

And no need, Jenna thought, for anyone to see a car with New York license plates in the driveway. "Thanks. That was good thinking."

"I realize what's at stake." Violet smiled and left it at that.

CHAPTER NINE

Though Jenna had slipped downstairs early that morning to enjoy a quick breakfast of French toast and bacon, Daniel wasn't as lucky. When he stirred shortly before noon, Jenna presented him with Violet's special broth with its odd combination of gingerroot, garlic and rosemary. To her surprise, he not only readily drank it, he kept the strange-smelling concoction—designed to heal and soothe—down.

Shortly after consuming the broth, Daniel walked to the bathroom with only standby assistance to take a shower. Jenna remained outside the door in case he became unsteady and called for help. He did fine, but the simple act appeared to exhaust him.

Instead of the interrogation she'd expected, Daniel immediately crawled back into bed and fell into a deep slumber.

As had become her custom, Jenna sat in the chair while he slept. She rested her head back and let her eyes drift shut. The feel of a hand on her arm had Jenna jerking upright.

Her racing heart slowed when she saw Violet with a bowl in her hands and a twinkle in her eyes. "Wake up, sleepyhead."

Putting a finger against her lips, Jenna rose and pointed to the door.

Jenna followed Violet into the hall. She left the door slightly open, wanting to hear Daniel if he stirred.

"I mixed up a paste of homemade aloe and eucalyptus for him." Violet kept her voice low, though not as low as Jenna might have wished. "Spread it on his chest."

Jenna gazed down into the bowl. "Looks…interesting."

"All natural ingredients, straight from the garden."

The last time Jenna had seen the plot of ground that Violet called a garden, it had been only weeds. And even with the weeds gone, could those plants even grow in Maryland? "Are you saying you got the aloe and eucalyptus from our garden?"

Violet smiled. "It may have a strong scent, but it's good stuff. Trust me, it's exactly what he needs."

"I do trust you." Jenna squeezed Violet's shoulder, the simple touch bringing a familiar surge of energy. "Thank you. Once he's awake—"

"I'm awake now."

The deep voice coming from the bedroom had Jenna freezing and Violet grinning.

Violet headed for the stairs, and after taking a breath, Jenna eased open the door and stepped into the room. She found Daniel sitting up in bed.

"You are awake." Jenna couldn't stop her smile. "And looking much, much better."

"I may be going out on a limb here, but I feel confident I'm going to live. Several times, I wasn't so sure." He chuckled, then puzzlement filled his eyes. "Can you tell me what I had? It had to be something big, because I can't recall ever feeling that bad."

Feeling awkward having a conversation while she was standing and he was in bed, Jenna dropped into the chair she'd vacated. She offered him an encouraging smile. "What do you remember?"

"Driving here."

She waited for him to elaborate. When he didn't, she gently pushed. "Anything else?"

Daniel's brows furrowed in concentration. "I remember half walking, half crawling up the stairs, feeling absolutely horrible. The last thing I remember was dropping down in front of the toilet bowl."

He settled his gaze on her, clearly looking to her to fill in the blanks.

"The answer isn't glamorous or particularly pretty." Jenna found herself fighting a smile. "You were brought to your knees by a simple stomach bug."

"I like the 'brought to my knees' idiom. It's quite appropriate in terms of how you found me." He appeared to be fighting a smile. "At least tell me this particular bug was a horrific one."

"On a scale of one to ten," Jenna paused for effect, "I'd put it at a twenty."

He grinned. "I've always been an overachiever."

Jenna found his boyish charm and good nature to be a potent combination. Still, she didn't want to make light of or downplay what he'd experienced. "You were very sick. This bug had to be a particularly virulent strain. The fact that you were in good physical health worked to your advantage."

"Good to know that those visits to the gym weren't in vain."

They exchanged a smile, then his expression turned serious. "You took excellent care of me. Because of you, I will live to write another day. Thank you. Sincerely."

"You're very welcome."

He studied her, likely taking in her unbrushed hair and shiny clean face devoid of any makeup. "I don't even know your name."

"It's Jenna."

"Jenna," he repeated before his curious green eyes once again settled on her face. "Who was that in the hall with you?"

"That was Violet. She loves gardening and is all about medicinal herbs." Jenna tipped the bowl so he could see the concoction

Violet had given her. "She brought me a poultice to apply to your chest."

Daniel's dark brows pulled together as he tried to process that. "So, you take care of the house, and that girl is the gardener?"

"Um-hmm," Jenna murmured. The last thing she wanted to do right now was get pulled into a discussion about her and Violet. "This is an aloe and eucalyptus paste. Is it okay if I rub it on your chest?"

"Do you think it's necessary?"

"I do." Jenna met his questioning gaze with a confident one of her own. Violet had said it was exactly what he needed. That was enough for her.

"You're the nurse," he said as if her endorsement was all he needed. Unexpectedly, he scrubbed his forehead with his hands, then expelled a frustrated breath. "I just woke up not that long ago, but I'm wiped. I'm going to close my eyes for a few minutes."

When his lids drifted shut, Jenna rose and moved to the bedside.

"I need to get these covers out of the way. I don't want to get paste on them." Jenna lowered the sheet and blanket to a spot just above the waistband of his pajamas.

He didn't acknowledge that he'd heard her. His eyes remained closed. Still, Jenna didn't want to presume. She continued to explain in low tones what she was doing.

"I'm going to get your pajama shirt out of the way as well." Her fingers made quick work of unfastening the buttons.

The various patterns on the vintage pj's never failed to make her smile. Today's pajamas sported burgundy sailboats on a cream-colored background.

Jenna rubbed her hands together to warm them before dipping her fingers into the paste. "I apologize if my hands are cold."

"S'fine," came his sleepy response.

His chest was broad and muscular with a light dusting of dark hair. The paste spread easily, and his skin held enough heat that, even if her fingers had been cold at the beginning, they wouldn't have stayed that way for long. Thankfully, the strong scent of the eucalyptus tempered the aloe's onionlike smell.

Applying it evenly and thoroughly took time. By the time she was done, Jenna had used every bit of the paste.

"You're going to be back to your old self in no time." She kept her voice soft and reassuring as she wiped her hands on a towel Violet had thoughtfully provided. She rebuttoned his shirt and pulled up the covers.

Once she'd washed the last of the paste from her hands, Jenna returned to the chair that had been her home for the past two nights. She'd been so worried about Daniel. Thankfully, based on the progress she'd seen today, she felt confident that a complete recovery was in sight.

Jenna knew the care she'd rendered had helped. She shuddered to think what might have happened if it had just been him in an otherwise empty house.

As happy as she was for him, Jenna experienced a twinge of sadness. Her time in this house was coming to an end.

With the day of reckoning approaching at lightning speed, Jenna moved an item she'd been pushing aside to the top of her mental to-do list.

She needed a get-out-of-GraceTown plan, stat.

"How is our favorite patient?" Rosemary asked when Jenna joined her and Violet for afternoon tea.

"He's sleeping now." Jenna's lips lifted in a weary smile as she gratefully accepted the steaming cup Violet handed her. "He took a shower this morning all by himself. I offered to help, but he insisted he felt strong enough."

"I heard the water running." Concern filled Rosemary's eyes. "Weren't you worried about him falling?"

Before answering, Jenna took a long sip of the Earl Grey. For the past three nights, she'd gotten little sleep and could definitely use the caffeine.

"Jenna?" Rosemary prompted.

"I'm sorry." Setting down her cup, Jenna expelled a breath. "It's been a crazy few days."

"You look exhausted." Violet studied her over the rim of her cup. "But also, I think, relieved."

"Daniel is much better, so I am relieved. Extremely relieved." Jenna shifted her attention back to Rosemary. "Just so you know, I waited outside the door while he showered in case there were issues, but he did just fine."

"You've taken stellar care of him." Rosemary bit into a fruit tart, her eyes bright with interest. "Did he tell you what had him showing up here out of the blue?"

"Until today, he's been too ill to say much." Jenna had the feeling that when he woke from his nap, he'd have more questions. Pointed questions. Ones for which she had no good answers. At least no answers she could give him that would excuse trespassing.

Violet pushed back her chair and stood.

"Where are you going?" Jenna asked.

"To work in the garden."

"As soon as I finish my tea, I'll join you," Rosemary called out.

"Sounds good." Violet reached for the doorknob.

"Violet. Hold up." Jenna knew she couldn't delay this discussion a second longer.

The girl turned, her lips curving upward ever so slightly. "What's on your mind?"

When their eyes met, something passed between them. Something that told Jenna that Violet already knew what she was about to say.

~

When his fever had broken early that morning, it had left Daniel soaked in sweat, but strangely feeling stronger. He hadn't even needed the nurse's assistance when he'd gotten up. She'd offered to help him in the shower, but he'd assured her he could manage.

Who knew taking a shower demanded so much energy? When he'd come out of the bathroom, he'd seen his bed linens had been changed, and fresh pajamas had been laid across the bed.

He'd slept, and then, after she'd rubbed that smelly stuff across his chest, Daniel had slept some more.

When he awoke now, his gaze went automatically to the chair against the far wall.

Only then did he realize he was alone.

Daniel had grown used to seeing the woman with the kind brown eyes in that chair whenever he opened his eyes. He remembered the cool feeling of the back of her hand against his feverish forehead and the worry that often clouded her eyes.

Daniel shifted his gaze to the window. The sunlight streaming in through the open blinds had him blinking, but for the first time in days, his eyes didn't hurt when the light hit them.

He moved his shoulders and arms and realized his joints and muscles no longer ached.

Daniel slowly sat all the way up. Glancing down, he realized the pajamas he'd pulled on after his morning shower, the ones with the geometric print design, had been his grandfather's favorite. He smiled, finding comfort in the memory and in the connection he felt being in this house his grandfather had loved.

Swinging his legs over the edge of the bed, he sat there for several seconds, making sure he felt steady enough to stand. It was what the nurse had made him do each time she'd helped him get up.

After showering and brushing his teeth, he found his clothes neatly folded in the dresser drawers. Though it felt amazingly good to shed the pajamas, simply pulling on shorts and a polo took effort.

His stomach growled.

How long had it been since he'd consumed more than soup and broth? For the first time since he'd arrived in GraceTown, Daniel felt confident that whatever he ate would stay down.

Not sure when the nurse would return, he decided to go in search of food. Standing at the top of the stairs, he heard the murmur of voices coming from the main level, all female.

Daniel recognized one as the nurse, another as the gardener. The other was unfamiliar.

He was too far away to make out what they were saying. When he reached the main floor, he paused to listen and realized the voices came from the kitchen.

Once he reached the living room, he could clearly hear the conversation.

"He's going to be angry and report us."

That was Jenna, the nurse. He'd know her voice anywhere. Why would she think he'd be angry?

"I believe he's going to see that we're helpful and ask us to stay."

Daniel was fairly certain that voice belonged to Violet, the gardener.

"Maybe he's just passing through. Or maybe he's hiding from something." Excitement filled the voice of an unfamiliar woman. "Maybe he's not the real Daniel Grace at all!"

Daniel chuckled and stepped into the doorway. "I wish I had your creativity."

An audible gasp arose from those seated at the kitchen table.

Three pairs of eyes focused on him.

"I assure you that I am the real Daniel Grace." He strode to the table, pulled out a chair and took a seat. "Now, the question is, who are all of you?"

CHAPTER TEN

"It's nice seeing you up and about. And definitely yes to getting acquainted." Rosemary smiled brightly. "But first, I'm betting you're ready to eat something more substantial than soup and broth."

After days spent in relative silence, Daniel appeared stunned by Rosemary's nonstop chatter. He blinked, then nodded. "I'll take any food you have to offer."

Rosemary brought a finger to her lips, then cocked her head. "How about a chicken sandwich and applesauce?"

Before Daniel could respond, Rosemary turned to Jenna. "Does that meet with your approval?"

"Daniel doesn't need my approval." Jenna offered her aunt a smile. "But toast, chicken and applesauce are all relatively bland and easy to digest."

Jenna looked at Daniel. "If your stomach feels settled, you should be okay to eat."

"Great." Daniel pushed back his chair. "I'll get it—"

"You sit." Using what Jenna thought of as her "motherly" voice, Rosemary motioned him down. "I know where everything is. While I do that, we can do as Daniel suggested and each tell a little about ourselves."

Jenna stifled a groan, then told herself to buck up and get this over with. She offered Daniel a smile. "I'll start. As you know, I'm Jenna. The woman at the toaster is my great-aunt, Rosemary. I'm a nurse, but I'm on sabbatical. We decided to take a road trip. It had been a while since we had a vacation."

Nerves made her stilted delivery sound even more choppy.

"We decided we'd go wherever the wind blew us." Rosemary smiled and set the sandwich in front of him. The plain-Jane chicken sandwich sat on one of the pretty china plates from the cupboard. She returned a moment later with a cup of applesauce.

He smiled his thanks.

If Daniel had noticed Jenna hadn't mentioned last names, it didn't show. He inclined his head. "And the wind blew you to GraceTown?"

"Same wind that blew you here," Violet piped up.

Rosemary tittered.

"Violet!" Jenna couldn't believe the girl's cheeky tone.

Daniel smiled. "You're right. I hadn't planned to come here, and this isn't a vacation for me. I'm here to finish my novel."

"Unplanned trips are the best." Rosemary, back at the table with a fresh cup of tea, offered a sage nod. "When we left home, we had no specific plans."

"Where's home?" Daniel lifted the sandwich and took a bite.

"Philadelphia," Rosemary answered promptly.

Everything in Jenna froze. Could this conversation get any worse?

"Great town. Lots of history." Daniel shifted his gaze to Jenna.

"We didn't get out much," Rosemary said before Jenna had a chance to change the subject. "Jenna worked two jobs, and the neighborhood we lived in, well, there was a lot of crime, and I didn't feel comfortable going out alone. When Jenna proposed we take this trip, and perhaps look for a new home base, I was on cloud nine."

"A trip that would take you wherever the wind blew." Daniel scooped up a spoonful of applesauce, his attention now fully focused on Rosemary.

"Exactly." Rosemary's eyes took on a distant glow.

For a second, Jenna thought—hoped—Rosemary would launch into one of the stories of her youth.

That hope was quickly shattered.

"I thought the wind might blow us farther." Rosemary paused. "Perhaps in a different direction. But I'm glad we landed here."

"I'm curious." Daniel offered Rosemary an encouraging smile. "How did you end up here, in my home?"

Before Rosemary could respond, Violet inclined her head, her expression thoughtful as she looked at Daniel. "Has it ever been your home?"

Confusion clouded his green eyes. "I don't follow."

"This was your Grandfather Frederick's home."

"Yes, and he willed it to me."

"The house is legally yours," Violet agreed. "But it's never been your home."

Two tiny lines formed between Daniel's brows. "Isn't that just semantics?"

"You're a writer. Do you believe anything is 'just semantics'?"

Daniel nodded good-naturedly. "Touché."

"There is a difference." Violet's voice remained conversational. "A house is a physical structure. A home is a sanctuary, a place where you feel you belong."

"Interesting take." Daniel studied Violet for a long moment, then waved a hand in the air. "However you twist it, this house is mine. And yet, somehow, you three ended up in it."

Before Jenna could jump in, Violet pushed forward. "Is that why you finally came here? You're searching for a place where you can rest, relax and be at peace?"

"I came here to write," Daniel told Violet. "That's what I do."

"You've been struggling." Violet spoke as if that was an accepted fact, not a guess. "You've come to the right place. You won't struggle here."

"I hope not." Daniel sipped his tea. "I'm still confused about what the three of you are doing here."

"You want more of the story?" Violet's blue eyes twinkled.

"I do." Daniel's full attention was now on Violet.

"Then I'll tell you."

"Violet, please," Jenna protested, having no idea how much the girl intended to reveal.

"Jenna." Violet's gaze met hers. "Daniel deserves the truth."

"Let me tell—"

"We came to GraceTown because of me," Violet said, cutting Jenna off. "We've told people I'm Jenna's sister, but that's not totally accurate in a strictly biological sense. Jenna was protecting my privacy. Until a few weeks ago, I was a ward of the state. That's how Jenna and I met. She worked at my group home. Anyway, when I aged out of system, I decided to come to Grace-Town. I needed a ride, so Jenna helped me."

Daniel appeared to be mulling over her revelation as he took another bite of the sandwich and chewed thoughtfully for several seconds. "You have family here."

He tossed out the statement as if there could be no other explanation.

"Nope." Violet smiled brightly. "No family here."

"But you used to?" Daniel pressed.

"I was here a long time ago. I knew about this house and the love that existed within its four walls." Violet's lips curved ever so slightly. "I knew when it was abandoned."

"This house wasn't ever abandoned," Daniel insisted.

"It certainly wasn't being loved." Violet didn't back down. "Not the way a house like this deserves to be."

"Violet, please," Jenna began.

"What? I'm only saying what's true. Daniel hires people to mow the lawn, clean and make sure the roof doesn't leak, but a house like this needs more. It needs people to care for it. To love it. That's who we are. People who care."

"Look, we honestly meant no harm." Jenna spoke quickly. "We just needed a safe place to stay, and we vowed to leave the house better than we found it."

"It's true," Rosemary, never one to stay quiet for long, chimed in. "Just ask the neighbors. They'll tell you we've been no trouble."

Daniel arched an eyebrow. "And these would be the neighbors who didn't think to call me when strangers moved into my house?"

"Well, in their defense, they think Jenna is your fiancée," Rosemary explained.

"They think what?" Daniel's voice rose, but he immediately pulled it down. "Why would they think that?"

"Well, because we told them so." Rosemary picked up the last bite of fruit tart from her plate and popped it into her mouth.

"Why would you do that?" Daniel spoke slowly, emphasizing each word.

"Okay, technically, I didn't tell them that Jenna was your fiancée," Violet gently clarified. "Only that you were getting married."

Jenna brought a hand to her head and inwardly groaned.

When Daniel set his sandwich back on the plate and opened his mouth to respond, Jenna jumped into the conversation.

"This is getting out of hand. Daniel, we're sorry. Now that you're better, we'll leave." Even though she'd told herself all along that this was what would happen once he recovered, Jenna still felt her heart twist at the thought of leaving.

"We have no place to go."

Jenna gave Violet a warning headshake. "That isn't his concern."

Daniel's curious gaze shifted to Jenna. "Why did you need a safe place to stay?"

Had she said *safe*? She must have said it, or why would he be asking? *No more lies,* she told herself. *Stick to the facts.*

"It was raining," Jenna said. "A bad storm. It had been a long drive, and my aunt—"

"Ever hear of a motel?"

Jenna hesitated. Daniel appeared more puzzled than angry. She looked away. "Like you, we were hoping for privacy. Peace."

Silence filled the kitchen for several long heartbeats.

His gaze shifted from her to Rosemary, then to Violet, before settling back on her. "Okay, you can stay."

"What?" Jenna couldn't have heard correctly...could she?

"You can stay," Daniel repeated. A tiny smile tugged at the corners of his mouth as if he found her obvious shock amusing.

Jenna finally found her voice. "Why? I mean, thank you, but why?"

"Let's just say I know about needing peace. You helped me a lot this weekend when you didn't have to. Plus, the house does look great, and it's not like there isn't room. And frankly, if there are people to look after the house and deal with the neighbors while I write, all the better. Besides, something tells me there is more to your stories than you're telling me, and I do love a good story."

"There's nothing more—" Jenna stopped. There was more. So much more.

Rosemary rose and gathered up his empty dishes. "Thank you, Daniel. Now, about the neighbors…"

Daniel dipped a spoon into the applesauce. "What about them?"

"I believe what Rosemary is saying," Violet smiled at the older woman, "is that if we announce to the neighbors that you and Jenna are no longer engaged, they'll have more questions. You'll never get any time to write with them badgering you." Violet's voice was all sweetness and innocence, and Daniel couldn't hide his amusement at the girl's moxie.

"You're probably right." He shrugged. "Okay, we'll let them think whatever you want—for now."

"That we're engaged?" Jenna couldn't believe what she was hearing.

Daniel smiled. "Works for me."

"We'll be the perfect houseguests," Rosemary promised. "You won't need to worry about a thing while we're here."

"Thank you, Daniel." Jenna wished Daniel knew how much this reprieve meant to her.

"Thank you for taking care of me while I was sick."

Violet offered Daniel a coy smile. "Jenna will make the perfect fiancée for you."

Daniel laughed and shook his head, casting a glance at Jenna. "Figures that the only way I can make a relationship work is to not know I'm in it."

Daniel's fingers flew across the keyboard as the scene in his mind came together on the page. He wasn't sure if it was simply being in a new place, the plant Violet had given him that was supposed to stimulate creativity or the magic of the antique desk he'd found in his grandfather's office—all he knew was that his writer's block had lifted.

He'd written more in the past three days than he had in the past three months. Good pages. Ones that might need a little fine-tuning before he sent them on to Calista, but they were definitely solid and propelling the story forward.

He was considering the next scene when his stomach growled. Loudly.

Glancing at his watch, Daniel realized he'd been sitting at his desk for four hours and hadn't eaten.

Deciding to grab something from the refrigerator, Daniel took the stairs to the main level. He paused momentarily at the base of the steps, finding the house uncharacteristically quiet. He'd grown used to hearing Rosemary in the kitchen, singing as she cooked, baked and whatever else anyone did in a kitchen.

Violet flitted in and out of the house, her face usually smudged with dirt from the garden that he'd had yet to go out and inspect.

Jenna, well, she was more than likely working in the basement. He'd gone down there yesterday and found her in the middle of moving a table. Despite her protests that she had it under control and that she didn't want him to tax himself since he'd recently been ill, he'd helped her.

He'd made it clear she should let him know if more heavy lifting was in her future. She might have made the promise, but he wasn't confident she'd follow through.

Jenna had that take-charge, I-can-do-it-myself attitude. Daniel recognized the trait because he saw it in himself.

After quickly downing a couple of chicken roll-ups he'd found in the refrigerator, Daniel made his way to the basement.

He noticed the floor around the washer and dryer had been recently scrubbed, and the area smelled like pine. The nearby wooden clothes rack that he remembered his grandmother using made him smile.

When he'd been driving here, Daniel had been unprepared for all the memories. The hanging baskets of brightly colored flowers on the porch hadn't been there in years, not since his grandmother died.

He only had to look at his grandfather's desk—the one where he now did his writing—to see the top covered with envelopes, papers and a container filled with jelly beans just for him.

Daniel would give anything to see that decorative green glass jar filled with jelly beans again.

Was that why he hadn't come back before now? Because he'd

known being here wouldn't be the same without his grandparents? Now that he was here, though, he found himself remembering all the joy this house had once held.

Being in the basement had him remembering all the games of hide-and-seek he'd played with his sibs and cousins. He smiled at the memories.

Daniel heard movement up ahead. Instead of calling out, he stepped deeper into the cavernous basement, took a turn to the right and came to an abrupt stop.

Jenna was on her hands and knees, scrubbing the floor. She looked up at the sound of his footsteps.

"You don't have to do that." Though Daniel knew she wanted to prove she was caring for the house, this was going too far.

Jenna sat back on her heels and tried to push a strand of chestnut hair out of her face with the back of her hand. "You're right. I could use a mop, but I think the floors get cleaner this way."

She'd obviously missed his point.

"Forget the hands and knees. If I want squeaky-clean basement floors, I'll hire someone."

Waving a dismissive hand, Jenna pulled to her feet and blew that stubborn strand of hair out of her eyes. "No need. It's done."

The satisfaction that ran through her words was reflected on her face. She glanced down at the concrete. "How does it look?"

It looked, Daniel thought, like a concrete floor. But the pride in her voice demanded a more positive response. "It looks extremely clean. Like you could eat off the floor."

"Yes, it does." Leaning over to drape the rag in her hand over the side of the bucket at her feet, Jenna straightened and smiled. "What do you need?"

"Nothing. I didn't mean to disturb you. I've been in my office all morning and came downstairs to get something to eat and—"

"I'm sorry. I can make you something. Meals today are my

responsibility. Rosemary and Violet had a late breakfast, then went to the market. I got caught up in cleaning and—"

"No worries." Daniel placed a hand on her arm. "I'm capable of feeding myself."

"It's no trouble, really. I can whip together—"

"You know, you look like you need a break as much as I do." Daniel smiled. "Let's go out for lunch."

CHAPTER ELEVEN

"This place is adorable." Jenna glanced around the outside seating area of the Black Apron Bistro, the café that Daniel had chosen for their lunch outing.

When he'd asked for her input on where to go, she'd told him the only places she'd been since arriving in town had been an antique store, a park and the market.

"My grandfather insisted we eat here every time I came to town." Daniel's lips curved. "It became a tradition."

Jenna fought a pang of envy. "Traditions are nice."

"They are." Daniel gazed expectantly at her. "Do you and your family have any traditions?"

Though he was likely only making conversation, Jenna searched for something that might qualify.

Just when she thought she was going to have to admit defeat and sound pathetic, she recalled one. "With my dad in the military, we moved a lot. Once we got settled in our new location, my mom and I would spend a day checking out the shops in town."

Moving aside the menu, Daniel gave her his full attention. "Did you buy something for your new home?"

Jenna shook her head, the happiness of the memory taking a

sharp dip. "There was more looking than buying. Anytime something caught my eye, my mother made sure to remind me that anything purchased would have to eventually be boxed up and moved or left behind in a couple of years."

Surprise flickered across Daniel's face. "You moved that often?"

"Six times before I graduated from high school. The last time was at the start of my senior year."

Daniel studied her for a long moment. "That had to be difficult."

Jenna wished she'd remained silent. She certainly didn't want Daniel, or anyone, feeling sorry for her. "I tried not to let myself get too attached."

Still, leaving had never been easy for her. Which was why she needed to remember that the Grace house, this town and her growing friendship with Daniel were temporary. And, for her sake and his, the less he knew about her life, the better.

Jenna picked up the menu. "What's good here?"

His gaze remained on her. "They're known for their crab cakes."

Jenna hoped they'd keep the conversation focused on the menu going forward. Or the weather. Or anything else equally inane and impersonal. No such luck.

"I'm sorry you had to move so often."

Her heart swelled at the sympathy in his voice. She vividly recalled her father's response anytime she'd asked if they *really* had to move *again*. There'd been no sympathy from the master sergeant, only a piercing look and an order to buck up.

Because the kids she'd known there talked about it, Jenna knew her father could have asked to stay where they were so she could finish her senior year. He wouldn't consider it.

When the silence lengthened, she realized that Daniel was expecting a response. "It's the life of the family of a career soldier. But you're correct, it can be difficult on the family."

She studied the eclectic menu, though none of the items really registered.

"How did you cope?"

"I read a lot. Books were my constant companions, no matter where we lived."

"What specific genres do you prefer to read?"

Daniel, Jenna was beginning to realize, possessed an insatiable curiosity.

Jenna opened her mouth to respond, but the arrival of their server disrupted the conversation.

"I'm sorry I kept you waiting." Sporting the café's classic black apron, the young man—Jax, according to his name tag—offered a friendly smile. "Do you have any questions for me about the menu?"

"I'm afraid we've been doing more talking than looking." Jenna gave the server a quick smile. "Could you give us five minutes? I promise I'll be ready when you come back."

"Take as much time as you need." Jax shifted his gaze from her to Daniel. "While you're perusing the menus, may I get either of you something other than water to drink?"

"Water works for me." Jenna might not have had to use any of the money she'd pulled out of savings for housing, but food for three was still making a dent.

"What are today's drink specials?" Daniel asked.

Jax consulted his notepad. "We have two today, a cranberry-basil spritzer and a rhubarb lemonade."

"The rhubarb lemonade sounds intriguing." Daniel glanced at Jenna.

"It does sound good." Jenna waved an airy hand. "You should give it a go."

"It's very popular," Jax said quickly. "We have people calling to find out when it will be offered next."

"Why don't you give us two of those," Daniel told him.

"Yes, sir. I'll be right back with your drinks." The boy hurried off before Jenna could reiterate that water was all she wanted.

Though this was no five-star restaurant, it was cute and trendy, and she had no doubt drinks wouldn't be cheap.

"If you don't like the taste, don't drink it," Daniel told her, obviously misinterpreting her expression. "Whenever my grandfather and I came here, we'd always try the most unusual drink special they had that day."

"I think it sounds amazing," Jenna admitted, then decided to lay it on the line. If she didn't, he might question why when she ordered only a side salad or whatever happened to be the least expensive item on the menu. "The thing is, I took money out of savings for this adventure with my aunt. I need to watch my pennies."

Understanding flickered in his green depths. "I'm sorry. I should have made it clear that this lunch is on me."

Jenna was already shaking her head, but he continued anyway.

"You took excellent care of me when I was sick. I have no doubt you skipped meals in order to watch over me. Tell me you didn't."

When he pinned her with his gaze, she could only shrug. "Just a couple, and I was happy to do it."

"Well, I'm happy to pay today."

Before Jenna could protest, Jax was back with their drinks.

Served on the rocks in a whiskey tumbler and garnished with lime, mint leaves and a stalk of rhubarb, the pink drink made a fetching picture.

"You're going to love it," Jax assured them.

"I'm sure we will," Daniel replied. "And I'll be picking up the check today."

Jenna opened her mouth, then closed it.

"Very well." Jax's gaze shifted from Daniel to Jenna. "Have you had time to look at the menu?"

Jenna could see the tables were full and knew that it wouldn't be fair to keep Jax coming back because of her failure to decide. "I'm ready."

"What can I get you?" Jax's pen poised above his order pad.

"The crab cakes," she told him. "With Old Bay fries for the side."

Daniel scooped up the menus and handed them to Jax. "Make that two."

"Good choice." Jax nodded approvingly. "The kitchen is pretty speedy today, so the wait for your food shouldn't be long."

Once Jax was out of earshot, Jenna focused on Daniel. "Thank you. I really didn't come here expecting you to pick up my lunch tab."

"If they're anything like I remember, you're going to love the crab cakes."

"I'm sure I will." Jenna took a deep breath and let the scent of grilled seafood, spicy fries and something sweet envelop her. "Everything smells so good here."

Daniel chuckled. "It really does."

She gave a laugh. "It's been so long since I went out for lunch, I feel like a kid in a candy store."

"With working two jobs, I'm surprised you had time for much of anything else."

"I managed to get out every now and then." Jenna kept her voice offhand, determined to change the subject. She latched on to something he'd said about his grandfather and this café.

"Did you and your grandfather come here often?"

His eyes took on a distant glow. "Every time I was in town."

"Was that often?"

"Usually at least twice a year, more often after Gram died." Sadness blanketed Daniel's face. "The two of them were insepara-ble. He said more than once that losing her was like losing half of himself."

The sentiment had a yearning rising up inside Jenna. "Do you ever wonder what it'd be like to have a love like that?" The fanciful thought sounded lame once she'd said it aloud. "You don't need to answer."

To her surprise, Daniel didn't laugh. "I've never come close to that feeling. But yes, I have wondered."

"Are you dating anyone?"

For some reason, the simple question appeared to take him by surprise.

"I just thought I'd ask because," she lifted her left hand and wiggled her bare ring finger, "engaged, you know."

"I forgot about that." He grinned. "I suppose it wouldn't do to have a jealous mistress showing up in town." Leaning forward, he dropped his voice to a conspiratorial whisper. "Then again, a little scandal might be exciting for the neighbors."

When Daniel wiggled his eyebrows like a cartoon villain, Jenna couldn't help but laugh. "It's just that I don't want to cause problems for you and anyone—"

"You're not causing any problems, I promise."

Jenna breathed a sigh of relief and took a sip of water.

"What about you? Any spurned ex-lovers I should be on the lookout for?"

She choked on her water.

After catching her breath and reassuring Daniel she was fine, she answered, "Definitely no ex-lovers. No time." She shrugged good-naturedly. "Two jobs."

His gaze remained firmly fixed on her face. "Surely, you found time to go out with friends or accept an occasional date."

Jenna nearly said that you didn't meet eligible men working as a private-duty nurse, but swallowed the impulse. Mentioning her work with Cherise would likely only lead to more questions. "I went out with friends occasionally, but it's been a while since I've dated."

"Was it serious with the last guy?"

There it was again, that curiosity well suited to a writer.

"Yes and no." Jenna absently took a sip of the drink sitting in front of her. "I liked Kevin, I really did. But I knew we weren't a good fit, not for the long run, anyway."

Curiosity flickered in Daniel's eyes. "Really?"

"He was in the military." Jenna's fingers tightened around the glass she realized she still held. "He loved the service."

"More than he loved you?"

"He graduated from the Naval Academy in Annapolis." To her, that said it all. "It was a mistake for us to even date."

"I understand the feeling." An odd look filled his gaze, but was gone so quickly Jenna wondered if she'd only imagined it. "I have another question for you."

The look in his eye put her on high alert. "What is it?"

"How did you explain away the lack of engagement ring to those here in GraceTown? It had to have come up."

Jenna blinked at the abrupt change in subject.

"It did come up," she admitted. "I simply said that all I've ever wanted was a simple gold band and love."

Daniel took a sip of the lemonade. He must have liked it, because he took a second, longer drink. "Is that true?"

He sounded skeptical, just like her friends had in the past when she'd told them the same.

"Yes." She met his gaze. "Absolutely true."

"Huh." He took another drink, then smiled when he saw her watching him. "Try another sip. It's an acquired taste."

"I liked it the first time." Still, she brought the glass to her mouth, paying attention to the way the tart and sweet flavors mixed on her tongue.

"Delicious," she pronounced, setting down the glass.

A dimple winked in his left cheek as his gaze shifted.

Jenna watched him take in the black-and-white-striped awning over the windows and the painted white façade with a red door. The bright red was a perfect contrast to the black and white.

The raised planters that separated the outdoor tables from the pedestrian walkway overflowed with flowers and greenery.

"This was Grandpa Fred's favorite café." Daniel's tone held a hint of sadness. "He and Ted, the owner, were friends. Whenever we were here, Ted would stop by the table to say hello."

"That kind of connection is nice." Jenna's tone turned wistful. "Rosemary has already started building a circle of friends here. It will be hard on her when it's time for us to leave."

Jenna wasn't sure what got into her. She reached across the table and covered his hand with hers. "Thanks for letting us stay a little longer."

"It's my pleasure."

Before he could say more, a portly older gentleman with salt-and-pepper hair approached the table with two plates of food, a broad smile on his face.

Jenna pulled back her hand.

The man set the plates on the table in front of them, his gaze fixed on her lunch companion. "Danny boy, it's been too long."

"Ted." Daniel rose and was immediately enfolded in a bear hug, complete with a couple of hard slaps on his back. "It's good to see you."

"When I heard you were here, I told Jax I'd bring out your food. This is like old times." For the first time, Ted's attention shifted to Jenna. "Only, instead of being here with your grandfather, I find you holding hands with your pretty fiancée."

The long pause that followed could have been awkward, except Daniel had turned to smile at Jenna before returning his attention to Ted. "How did you know? About the fiancée part?"

"Ah, Danny, you know that GraceTown in many ways is still a small town."

Daniel nodded as if accepting the truth of the statement. "Well, it's high time you and Jenna met. Ted Boczanski, I'd like to introduce you to Jenna…"

He hesitated for a barely perceptible beat, and Jenna realized he didn't know her last name. Obviously, that lack of knowledge hadn't registered until now. Which meant she needed to be prepared when it came up again. She'd deal with that situation later, when she didn't have Ted smiling at her.

Jenna rose and extended her hand. "It's a pleasure to meet you, Mr. Boczanski. Daniel was just telling me how you always made a point of coming over when he and his grandfather ate here."

"Fred was a friend. A good one." The smile that played at the corners of Ted's lips lingered for a second, then faded. "A wonderful man."

"I wish I could have known him." Jenna meant every word. Being in Fred's house had made her wonder about the man who'd made it a home. "From what Daniel has told me, he sounds like a remarkable person."

"He was." Ted gestured with his head toward Daniel. "You've got yourself a good one here."

Jenna smiled at Daniel. "I can vouch that he's strong and determined."

She was referring to the way he'd fought his recent illness, but Ted had another take on the comment.

He threw back his head and laughed. "Sounds like she gave you a run for your money, Danny boy."

"The effort was worth it. Jenna is one of a kind."

Jenna wasn't sure what to think when Daniel reached over and, taking her hand, brought it to his lips.

"Your grandfather would be thrilled to see you so happy." Ted cleared his throat. "It's great to have you back, and I hope you come by often." Ted refocused his attention on Jenna. "I hear your family is here with you. Next time you're out and hungry, I hope you'll bring them by. I'd love to meet them."

"I'll do that, thank you."

Once Ted left, Jenna fully expected Daniel to bring up the subject of her last name, but the food was on the table, and as they sat down to eat, a kid rode by on a scooter, prompting Daniel to start telling her about the skateboard he'd had as a boy...until he'd fallen off it and broken several bones in his hand.

"Those things can be dangerous." Jenna gave a little shudder. "Did your hand heal without any issues?"

"Good as new." Lifting his right hand, Daniel wiggled his fingers. "If it wasn't, I'd be dictating my current work in progress."

"How did you get started writing?" Jenna asked, genuinely curious.

"Are you telling me you haven't already looked up that information?" he asked with a teasing smile.

Actually, she had. Of course she had. What was the point in denying it? She offered him a sheepish smile. "I may have done a search or two."

He inclined his head.

"You have a lovely website. Your publisher also has a lot of stuff out there on you, but I'm a big fan of firsthand information."

Daniel picked up a seasoned fry. "Because what is printed can be slanted?"

"Or even untrue." Jenna thought about what might be said about her incident with Michael Menard in the press. She had no doubt it would be slanted—and all of it untrue.

"What's out there—on the official sites—is accurate." He finished off one fry and picked up another. "I started out my professional life as an attorney. Now, much to my family's chagrin, I'm a novelist."

His tone might have remained light, but Jenna picked up on an undercurrent. It was likely the way she sounded when talking about being part of a military family.

"They wish you were still practicing law." She spoke as if it was a fact, because that was the sense she was getting.

"They do." Daniel's tone remained matter-of-fact. "My

parents are supportive, I don't want to give the impression in any way that they're not, but…"

When the silence lengthened, she prompted, "But?"

"The novel that sold wasn't the first I'd written. I wrote several others before that one. I view those novels as my training ground." His lips curved up. "The one that hit number one on the *New York Times* list—"

"The one that got optioned for a movie," Jenna added.

"Yes. That one, and the others that preceded it, were written when I was working full time, which in lawyer talk is really eighty billable hours a week."

"How did you do that?"

"No life." He chuckled. "At all. I didn't mind, because the story came alive, and I loved it. I got an agent, she shopped it around, it went to auction, and the rest is history."

"After that success, you quit being an attorney and became a full-time writer."

"I'm still an attorney," Daniel corrected. "I'm just not actively practicing right now."

Something in the way he said *right now* had Jenna cocking her head. "Are you planning to go back?"

"I have no plans at the present." He studied her. "Are you planning to go back to nursing?"

Jenna didn't want to talk about her life. But somehow, Daniel had once again circled the conversation back to her.

She forced an upbeat tone and added a smile. "Who said I ever left it?"

He stroked his chin. "You're not working now."

"I'm on a sabbatical right now, remember?" Jenna lifted her glass and took a long drink, buying herself some time.

Daniel appeared to brush the explanation aside. "Does you not working have to do with you and your family needing a safe place to stay?"

The sky that had been a brilliant blue earlier now held clouds, and the wind held a moist chill.

Gooseflesh popped up, and Jenna wrapped her arms around herself. "It feels as if a storm is coming. Once we finish eating, we should start back."

CHAPTER TWELVE

As they headed home after eating, they'd gone only a block when Daniel smiled and lifted a hand in greeting.

Jenna didn't recognize the woman walking down the sidewalk toward them with long, confident strides. She wore a suit, in sharp contrast to the casual way Jenna and Daniel were dressed.

A stylish suit, to be sure, with a thin, pencil skirt and trim, fitted jacket. Though she couldn't have been more than a few years older than Jenna, she appeared older.

It might have been the blond hair pulled ruthlessly back in an elegant chignon, but Jenna thought it had more to do with the woman's take-charge demeanor.

Yet, when she reached Daniel, the woman offered a bright smile and held out both hands.

Daniel immediately took them, his voice warm with welcome as he brushed a kiss across her cheek. "Annie, how long has it been?"

"I believe the last time was at your grandfather's funeral." A shadow passed over the woman's face. "I know Fred was in his eighties when he passed, but I honestly expected him to make it to a hundred. He was such a strong, vital man. Then he was gone."

"It was a shock to everyone in the family, but it hit me especially hard." Daniel blew out a breath. "I'd just seen him the weekend before."

A blessing that he'd come when he had, Jenna thought, recalling his comment about visiting only twice a year. Still, a memory tinged with regret came to her as she thought of her own parents and all they'd left unsaid.

If only you had a crystal ball that would tell you that this was the last time you'd ever see your loved one...

"You left his house empty for so long." Annie's gaze searched Daniel's face. "I was beginning to think you were going to sell it."

Daniel shook his head. "I could never do that. The house has been in the Grace family since it was built."

"I'm glad to hear that." Annie slanted a glance at Jenna. "When I heard your fiancée and her family had moved in, it gave me hope. Now, here you are." The woman held out her hand to Jenna. "Anne Laggett. It's a pleasure to meet the woman who captured Daniel's heart."

The phrase had Jenna wondering if the woman had a romantic side. If she did, it was well hidden.

Taking the proffered hand, Jenna returned the firm handshake with a firm one of her own. "I'm Jenna. It's nice to meet one of Daniel's friends."

"The Laggetts are one of GraceTown's founding families," Daniel explained to Jenna before refocusing on Anne. "Are you still working for the company?"

Surprise flicked in Anne's blue depths. "Of course."

"They're lucky to have you."

"I like to think so." Anne's gaze shifted from Daniel to Jenna before returning to him again. "What brings you two out on this gloomy day?"

Daniel smiled. "We had lunch at the Black Apron."

"I love their food." Anne smiled. "Unfortunately, I don't get there too often."

"Ted would love to see you."

"I know." Anne expelled a breath. "I'll make time one of these days."

Though Daniel appeared perfectly comfortable interacting with his old friend, Jenna suddenly remembered one of the reasons he'd allowed her and her family to stay was so they could run interference with those in the community.

"The crab cakes were fabulous," Jenna offered, drawing Anne's attention back to her. "If you get a chance—and it's still available —I can also vouch for the rhubarb lemonade. It was amazing."

"Thanks for the tip." Anne smiled at Jenna. "Are you in publishing?"

"Jenna is a nurse." Pride radiated in Daniel's voice.

"For some reason, I thought the woman you were dating was in publishing." Anne's brow furrowed, then she waved a dismissive hand. "Obviously, I was mistaken."

Jenna wondered if the woman Daniel had recently split with was also an author.

"What kind of nursing do you do?" Anne asked, sounding genuinely interested.

Jenna wasn't about to mention her private-duty care, and to mention her stint working in group homes might pull in Violet, so she went back a few years. "I started my career working on a medical-surgical floor at a hospital, then eventually went into hospice care."

"Did you like that?" Anne inclined her head. "I would think that dealing with death every day would be emotionally difficult."

"I found it very rewarding. I loved getting to know the patient and their family and doing what I could to make a difficult time easier." While Jenna had enjoyed caring for Cherise, talking about her work in hospice care made her realize how much she missed it. "Being there during the highs and lows of someone's life is a privilege."

"The world needs more people like you."

The admiration in Anne's blue eyes and the sincerity in her voice warmed Jenna's heart. "Thank you. That's kind of you to say."

Jenna didn't know what to think when Daniel reached over, took her hand and gave it a squeeze. "Jenna is an amazing woman."

Though she knew the sweet gesture was only for show, her heart didn't get the message. It became a heavy mass in her chest, and she had to resist the urge to sigh.

"Well, I'll let you get back to your stroll." Anne's voice suddenly turned all business. "It was good seeing you again, Daniel. Jenna, a pleasure."

"She seems like a nice woman." Jenna watched Anne stride down the sidewalk as if she owned it.

"Annie is a business powerhouse." Daniel's lips curved. "Grandpa Fred always said if you want something done, ask Annie." His gaze settled on Jenna. "I have the feeling if you and he'd had a chance to meet, he'd have said the same thing about you."

"That's nice of you to say." Jenna hadn't known she would ask the question until it rolled off her tongue. "Did you and Anne ever date?"

"While I like and admire Annie, the feelings I have for her have always been simply those of a friend."

Jenna understood. "Like you and me."

Daniel's only response was to gesture to a rapidly darkening sky. "Shall we call an Uber or take our chances?"

∽

Still laughing and more than a little out of breath from the sprint, Daniel pulled the door to the house shut behind them.

"Perfect timing," he pronounced as rain began to hammer against the roof.

"Only because we ran full out that last block." Jenna shook her head, and he could see the beads of moisture not only on her skin, but on the dark strands of her hair.

Once droplets had begun to fall, making thick plops against the sidewalk, Daniel had looked at Jenna. Getting a nod, he'd grasped her hand, and they'd taken off running.

The house had been in sight when they'd started laughing. Daniel couldn't recall the last time he'd tried to outrun the rain.

He hated that their time together today had been cut short. Then he reminded himself that she lived here, and so did he, so it wasn't as if he were dropping her off, and they'd have to make plans to see each other again.

The thought cheered him.

"I need to head upstairs and hit the keyboard," he told Jenna.

"I'm going to change into something dry and see if Rosemary needs any help."

"Doing?"

Jenna sniffed the air. "Are you familiar with Loaves of GraceTown?"

Daniel shook his head as the slightly sweet, yeasty aroma wrapped around him. "Doesn't sound familiar."

"One of Beverly and Geraldine's neighbors, Hannah Rogan, was at the party at their house and—"

"The party you attended the night I arrived."

"That's the one. Well, Hannah apparently told Rosemary about the program. While you were ill, my aunt contacted the coordinator."

Daniel studied her face, but saw nothing there. Still, something in her voice gave him pause. "You wish she hadn't."

"What?"

"You don't think Rosemary should have made that call."

Jenna hesitated for a long moment, then held up her hands, palms out. "I want to be very clear. I believe in volunteering and in helping those in need. That wasn't the issue."

Daniel offered an encouraging smile.

"At the time, we were living here without your permission. Then there was the matter of the cost of the ingredients. Though nominal, we still have limited funds." Jenna glanced out the window, then her gaze returned to Daniel. "Rosemary has difficulty remembering that we are only in GraceTown temporarily. I wasn't sure it was wise for her to make promises she might not be able to keep."

"Oh, so you're one of those."

Though Daniel kept his tone teasing, Jenna frowned.

"One of what?"

"A person who, if they say they're going to do something, they follow through."

Two tiny lines formed between her brows. "Aren't you?"

He noticed she did that a lot—automatically shifted the focus back to him. "I am a man of my word."

Daniel nearly smiled, but sensed that might make her think he was joking. He wasn't. That's why he'd been so stressed about his rapidly approaching deadline. He'd promised to deliver and was determined to make that happen.

"What are Loaves of GraceTown?"

"A group that provides bread to the food bank to pass on to people experiencing food insecurity," Jenna explained. "I discovered that volunteers often drop in and out of the program, and that's okay."

Daniel stroked his chin. "Seems like a lot of work when there are likely lots of day-old bread available from supermarket donations."

"Rosemary believes homemade bread is special, and that

getting a loaf of something freshly made especially for you says you're important."

"Not everyone would see it that way."

"You don't." There was no condemnation in her observation.

"Give him time."

Violet's voice had them both turning. "I believe Daniel is going to find that having us around is going to change him in more ways than he can imagine."

Daniel chuckled. "That change has already begun."

Jenna shifted to face Violet. "Seeing those dry clothes tells me you came in from the garden before the rain started."

Violet glanced down at her shorts and T-shirt and shrugged.

Jenna gestured with one hand to her damp dress. Her lips tipped in a rueful smile. "Daniel and I had to run the last block, and we still didn't make it before it rained on us."

"I have a suggestion." Violet leaned close. "Next time, slow down and savor the moment."

Violet's flippant tone brought a smile to Daniel's lips.

Jenna laughed. "Says the woman with the perfectly dry clothes."

"I don't mind a little rain." Daniel had never purposely walked in the rain. Now, standing beside Jenna, it sounded rather appealing.

A gust of wind suddenly brought a torrent of rain against the front window.

Jenna shook her head. "Yeah, I can see where walking in that would be loads of fun."

Violet's blue eyes danced with merriment. "I'm just saying, don't knock it until you've tried it."

"Ah, no, thank you." Jenna's droll tone had them chuckling. Then she turned to Daniel and playfully pointed at him. "You need to get upstairs and write. I have kept you away from your keyboard long enough."

"Yes, ma'am." As he climbed the stairs with the scent of fresh-baked bread wafting in the air, Daniel couldn't stop a smile.

When his grandfather was alive, this house had been filled with laughter and joy. Now it was again.

Thanks to his fake fiancée, her great-aunt and her sister.

Jenna strolled into the kitchen, expecting to find Rosemary at the stove. Instead, she found a note from her aunt, saying that she and Margaret were dropping off the loaves they'd baked then stopping at the senior center for bingo.

Her gaze was drawn to what appeared to be a last-minute addition scrawled at the bottom of the note:

The bread cooling on the rack is for dinner. HANDS OFF.

The note, so classic Rosemary, had her smiling.

Glancing around the large and spotless kitchen, Jenna was seized with the urge to follow in Rosemary's footsteps and make something special for everyone tonight.

A dessert, she thought. A pie. Everyone loved pie, and the Granny Smith and Honeycrisp apples she'd picked up at the market earlier this week would be the perfect combination of tart and sweet.

As Jenna gathered the ingredients she would need, she found herself humming. How long had it been since she'd simply taken the time to make a pie?

When it had been just her and Rosemary, a whole pie had seemed too much work. Tonight, there would be four people enjoying food and conversation around the dinner table.

Like a family, Jenna thought.

It was strange to think that if not for the incident with Michael Menard, she wouldn't be standing here now in this beautiful kitchen, setting out a glass pie plate and a mixing bowl as well as the necessary utensils.

Opening the refrigerator to get butter, Jenna did a quick boogie dance when she saw a box of refrigerated piecrust. She immediately removed it and placed it on the counter, then set the oven to 425 degrees.

Though she thought she remembered how to make a crust from scratch—and if she faltered, she could easily look it up online—this would be much faster.

While peeling the apples, she let her thoughts drift. Had it really been less than a month since they'd left Philadelphia? Right now, with the sunlight streaming through the windows, her life there seemed ages ago.

Really, it had been more of an existence than a life, she now realized. Working all those hours with no time for herself or her aunt. And for what? So they could live paycheck to paycheck?

Not quite true, she reminded herself, because the pittance she'd made from her second job had gone into their emergency fund. A fund that thankfully had financed their trip to Grace-Town and a whole new life.

Jenna already knew that, if by some miracle the charges against her were dismissed or a jury found her not guilty, she wouldn't return to Philadelphia. She would look for a job in a town like this one. A community where the air was fresh and clean and where a woman could walk alone without fear. A place where she and Rosemary could make friends and have a full life.

The truth was, if Jenna had her preference, she would stay here, but she knew that wouldn't be possible. Not after putting herself out there as Daniel's fiancée.

Once Daniel decided he wanted his house back, or maybe found someone he wanted to date—that thought brought a swift pang in the area of her heart—or if she learned that the police were actively looking for her, she and Rosemary would have to leave.

She would do her best to get Violet to go with them, but wasn't sure that would happen.

Jenna found herself unexpectedly blinking back tears as she moved to the other counter to press the dough firmly against the side and bottom of the pie plate.

She didn't want to leave GraceTown or this house or Daniel, but she would have no choice. Just like all those times as a child, she would simply have to buck up.

It was a good thing she'd had plenty of experience.

Jenna shoved the self-pitying thoughts aside. She would not let thoughts of the future ruin this afternoon. She would follow Violet's suggestion. She would slow down and savor this moment.

A little over an hour later, Jenna gazed admiringly at her masterpiece sitting on the cooling rack. Not only did it smell terrific, it looked just as good with the golden-brown crust sporting scalloped edges.

Jenna inhaled the sweet smell of apples, cinnamon and nutmeg and smiled.

"Something smells—" Daniel skidded to a stop in the doorway. "Whoa." His gaze slid from the pie to her. "Did you make that yourself?"

"I did." Jenna lifted her hands and wiggled her fingers. "With my own two hands."

"I could smell the enticing aroma all the way upstairs." He moved to the counter. "Can I have a piece?"

Jenna shook her head. "I'm afraid I just took it out of the oven. It needs to cool for a couple of hours before we cut into it."

"Seriously?"

She nodded. "I thought we'd have it for dessert tonight. Will you be staying in?"

"Ah, pie on the menu…" He gave a little laugh. "Let me consult my social calendar. It appears I'm free. You?"

"I just happen to also be available."

He grinned, and she found herself basking in the warmth of his smile.

Jenna glanced at the clock. "Rosemary said in her note she should be home from bingo by six, but I'm a little hungry now. Would you like to share some hummus and carrot sticks with me?"

Daniel cast one last longing look at the pie, then expelled a heavy breath. "I guess."

"Crunchy carrots, creamy hummus, yum." Jenna put some enthusiasm into her voice and stepped to the refrigerator.

"Don't bother to oversell it," he said, as if resigned to his fate. "We both know that while hummus and carrots are an okay snack, they can't compete with a piece of apple pie straight from the oven."

Agreeing and knowing this was one argument she couldn't win, Jenna scooped hummus onto two plates and added carrot sticks before looking up. "Inside or out?"

He shot her a teasing smile "Oh, so now I get a choice?"

"Hey, I'd love a piece of that pie as much as you, but do you know what would happen if I cut it now?"

Daniel shook his head.

"The filling would be runny. It needs time to thicken and set, for the flavors to meld together. Letting it cool also prevents the crust on the bottom from getting soggy from the hot filling."

Daniel made a face. "So you're saying a crusty bottom is better than a soggy bottom?"

Jenna laughed. "Actually, I'm saying a dry bottom is a tasty bottom."

"Can't argue with that. Let's sit outside on the porch, then." Daniel inclined his head. "Want to split a beer with me?"

"Sure."

Moments later, they were sitting on the porch, sipping an IPA and crunching on carrots dipped in hummus.

Jenna waved a carrot in the air. "This has turned out to be a stellar day."

"It really has." Daniel relaxed back against the wicker chair and took a long drink of beer. The sky was a vivid blue, and the sweet scent from the flowers in the hanging baskets filled the air.

"Did you get a lot of writing done this afternoon?"

Satisfaction blanketed his face. "I did. I can't believe how well it's going. Though I admit I keep waiting for the other shoe to drop."

Jenna stilled. That's what she had been doing, waiting for the police to show up at the door and for her life to implode. But Daniel? "I'm not sure I understand."

"The story is flowing, but it took so long to happen, I keep waiting for the words to dry up."

"You can't do that." Jenna set her plate on the wicker table and laid her hand on his. "Worrying will only steal your joy. Besides, you have talent. You must trust that talent."

"What about you?"

Puzzled, Jenna gave a little laugh. "What about me?"

He snapped a carrot stick in two, his gaze firmly fixed on her face. "What do you do when you find yourself worrying about something that may or may not happen?"

While this might be just a simple conversation over a beer, he deserved an honest answer. "I tell myself that I am a survivor. That whatever happens to me, I can handle it. My worries are more about Rosemary. If, for some reason, something does happen to me, and I'm unable to be there for her, I don't know how she'll survive. That's what can keep me up at night."

He didn't dismiss her concerns by mouthing some platitude, but appeared to carefully consider what she'd said.

"I think Rosemary is stronger than you give her credit for." When Jenna opened her mouth, he lifted a staying hand. "But I want you to know that, if anything should happen to you, I will take care of her. I will make sure she has what she needs and is okay."

She knew he meant what he was saying, and the relief, well, Jenna was just glad she was sitting down. For several seconds, the lump in her throat made speaking difficult. She finally found her voice. "Why would you do that? You barely know us."

"I know enough." His gaze met hers. "If there is anything I can do to save you from any misfortune, all you need to do is ask."

Jenna gave a jerky nod and swallowed once more. "Daniel."

"Yes, Jenna?"

She met his questioning gaze with a steady one of her own. "My last name is Woodsen."

CHAPTER THIRTEEN

Dinner that night was simple—hearty vegetable soup and crunchy sourdough bread with apple pie a la mode for dessert. Conversation was lively as they sat around the polished table in the dining room and discussed their day.

Listening to Violet talk about the plants she hoped to add to the garden had Jenna remembering these same kinds of conversations around her family's kitchen table growing up. Her mother had loved plants.

"My father thought hanging baskets and cultivating flower beds were wastes of time and money," Jenna found herself saying.

"Your father was a pragmatic man," Rosemary admitted. "A good man, but Larry viewed plants and flowers as extra, unnecessary work."

"My mom didn't agree." Jenna's lips curved the way they always did when she thought of her mother. "She believed plants were an easy way to bring color and warmth into our life. I agree with her."

"What about your parents, Daniel?" Rosemary shifted her focus from her soup to Daniel. "Did either of them have a green thumb?"

"I'm not sure." Daniel's brows drew together as he thought about it. "Our house was certainly surrounded by blooming plants and bushes, but the lawn crew oversaw planting and maintaining. Inside, there were always various floral arrangements, but I believe one of the staff took care of ordering those."

"That's cool."

Three pairs of eyes turned to Violet.

Violet raised her eyebrows. "What?"

"I thought you'd be of the mind that those in the household should be the ones digging in the dirt and doing the arranging," Daniel said.

"Your family employed people whose job it was to keep your lawns beautiful. The same with the plants inside." Violet still appeared slightly puzzled. "It doesn't matter who brings the beauty into our lives, just that we take time to recognize and enjoy it."

Jenna glanced at Daniel, realizing for the first time just how different his upbringing had been from hers. When she shifted her gaze from him to find Violet staring, Jenna flushed. It was almost as if Violet was reading her thoughts.

"What do you like most about being back in GraceTown?" Violet asked Daniel.

"I bet he likes the quiet," Rosemary said before he could answer. "New York City can be loud. When we lived in Philadelphia—"

"Aunt Rosemary, give the man a chance to answer." Jenna softened her words with a laugh. At least she hoped it softened them. She didn't like to interrupt, found it dreadfully rude, in fact, but she didn't want Rosemary giving out information about their life prior to GraceTown.

If Daniel noticed the awkwardness, he didn't let it show. Swallowing his bite of pie, he turned toward Rosemary to respond. "You're right, GraceTown is a lot quieter than New York City. But the place where I was living was well insulated, and the street it was on had little traffic, relatively speaking. We barely noticed the noise."

"We?" Rosemary leaned forward in her chair. Casting a not-so-subtle glance at Jenna, she asked, "Did you not live alone? You had a roommate?"

This time, it was Daniel's turn to laugh awkwardly. "I mean 'we' as in me and the voices in my head. My characters. Not actual voices."

Rosemary opened her mouth to ask more questions, but Violet beat her to it.

"I ask again: What do you like most about being back?" Violet appeared unwilling to let the subject drop.

Daniel rubbed his chin, and a thoughtful look filled his eyes. "I'd forgotten how much GraceTown—and this house—feels like home to me."

Violet then fixed her blue eyes on Rosemary. "What do you like most about living here?"

"It feels like a real home." Rosemary's wrinkled face lit up. "I never thought I'd have that again. You know, a real house, a front porch with chairs for rocking…"

A teasing glint filled Violet's eyes. "A handsome beau living just down the street."

"A what?" Jenna's apple-laden fork froze midway to her mouth. "You've met a man?"

"Mr. Whitehead and I are neighbors. And don't sound so shocked. I'm old, not dead."

"I don't know too many neighbors who stop over with a box of chocolates." Violet shot Rosemary an impish smile.

"Smoooooth," Daniel crooned, shooting a wink at Rosemary.

Jenna widened her eyes. "Barry Whitehead brought you chocolates?"

"A huge box," Violet informed Jenna. "What I'd like to know is, where's my piece?"

Rosemary laughed and shook her head.

Jenna couldn't recall her aunt ever looking happier.

"What about you, Jenna?"

Jenna shifted her gaze to Violet. "Yes, I'd like a piece of chocolate, too."

Laughter rippled around the table.

"I'm not talking about chocolate, although it's a great subject any time of day." Violet studied Jeanna from under a sweep of lashes. "What do you like best about living here?"

The question wrapped around Jenna's heart and squeezed tightly. It would be difficult to pick just one thing she liked best. Her time here had shown her all she'd been missing by working two jobs and having no free time.

Only now did she realized that in her quest to provide for her aunt, she'd failed them both. Even as regret lay heavy around her shoulders, she tried to assuage the guilt by telling herself that her intentions had been pure.

"It's hard sometimes," Rosemary's soft voice broke the lengthening silence, "to pick just one thing."

Jenna met her aunt's gaze, and the love that flowed between them was a strong bond capable of withstanding anything that tried to break it. "What I like most about living here is seeing you so happy. You being happy is all I've ever wanted."

Tears flooded Rosemary's eyes as she reached across the table and covered Jenna's hand with hers. "I feel the same about you."

For a second, Jenna was convinced that all the women around the table were going to dissolve into tears. Then she realized there was one person they hadn't heard from yet.

"Violet, you haven't told us what you like best."

"That's easy." Violet smiled. "Helping to change struggling into thriving."

An odd comment, Jenna thought.

Before she could probe further, Rosemary pushed her chair back with a clatter. "Who'd like a second piece of pie?"

~

On Friday, there were kabobs on the grill for dinner. As it was Violet's turn to clear the table and Rosemary's to load the dishwasher, that left Jenna lingering on the back patio with Daniel.

The like-new monster grill had performed admirably, and Jenna had no doubt it would be pulled into service again very soon.

"I remember when Grandpa Fred had this delivered." Daniel stared at the unit. "It wasn't long before he passed away."

"I'm sure he'd be glad to know you're putting it to good use." Jenna gently closed the lid. "This is a top-of-the-line model. We used to grill a lot when I was growing up, but none of our grills were ever as nice as this one."

"I can't believe you had to show me how to fire this up." Daniel's lips lifted in a self-deprecating smile. "Who doesn't know that?"

"Maybe a guy who has never been around one before?" Jenna knew he'd been embarrassed when she'd had to show him even the basics, so she kept her tone light. "I predict by the end of the summer you'll be a master griller. You're already halfway there now."

"I don't know about that." He chuckled. "But at least I know now how to get it going and how to adjust the settings."

"That's the spirit." She smiled up at him, then had to look away when their eyes met and her heart rate skyrocketed.

"Would you like to take a walk?" he asked abruptly. "I got a lot of work done today, and I'm ready to enjoy this gorgeous evening."

"I'd like that, too." Jenna cocked her head. "Any particular destination in mind?"

"Not really."

"I can do spontaneous." She smiled. "But let's tell the others that we're leaving. Maybe Rosemary and Violet will want to join us."

They stepped inside to find the dishwasher going and Rosemary and Violet standing at the counter, talking.

"Daniel and I thought we'd take a walk," Jenna informed the two. "Why don't you and Violet join us? It's so beautiful outside."

"I believe I'm going to stay home and relax. I might go for a stroll a little later." Rosemary smiled. "You have fun."

"What about you, Violet?" Jenna asked.

"Are you headed in the direction of Leaves of Green?" Violet asked.

Daniel brought the location of the popular garden center into focus. "We can be."

"Then I'll come." Violet reached for the small backpack she used as a purse. "I want to pick up a few plants for the garden."

Rosemary offered an indulgent smile. "You spend more time in that garden than you do in here."

"It's my happy place," Violet admitted. "And I wouldn't talk if I were you. When you're not playing bingo and gallivanting all over town with your friends, you spend a lot of time out there, too."

"You're right. Gardening has become a passion." Rosemary smiled. "Just seeing how quickly it's changed from a mass of weeds into a thriving garden is like, well, it's a miracle."

"A miracle that involved lots of hard work," Jenna reminded them. "I know how much time both of you have devoted to that patch of land."

Daniel cast Violet a questioning look. He'd meant to check out the garden, but had been so focused on his writing he hadn't gotten there. "I'd love to see what you've done so far."

"You're welcome anytime." Violet shot him a smile.

Jenna turned back to Daniel. "Do you want to see it now or…?"

"Let's do it tomorrow," Violet responded. "The nursery closes early tonight, which means we need to get going."

Jenna shifted her attention back to Rosemary. "We won't be long."

"Take all the time you want." Rosemary's blue eyes sparkled. "No need to rush home."

Once they reached the sidewalk, Daniel turned to the right, in the direction of Leaves of Green. Jenna's hand on his arm had him pausing.

"I just realized this is also the way to the River Walk and the town square." Her gaze searched his. "We may run into people you know or who know you."

"I'm not trying to avoid anyone," he said. "While finishing the novel is my priority, that doesn't mean I can't be social."

They took a few more steps, then a thought struck him. It seemed unlikely, especially considering that she'd attended a party the night he'd arrived in GraceTown, not to mention having lunch with him at the Black Apron. "Unless you prefer to avoid the locals?"

"No, but thanks for asking." She shot him a smile. "I love the town square with all the flowers and greenery. I've seen the River Walk, but only a quick glance."

"Pick up the pace, people," Violet urged. "This isn't a parade."

Laughing, Daniel moved from a stroll to a brisk walk. Beside him, Jenna did the same.

They had walked close to a half mile when Jenna skidded to a stop. "Oh no."

Daniel glanced around, trying to see the cause of her distress, but finding nothing amiss. "What's wrong?"

"There." Jenna pointed to an obviously injured bird lying on the grass near the curb.

"It's an oriole," Violet announced. "A male."

"You're right." Daniel took a few steps closer to the bird with its full black hood and vibrant orange chest, and sympathy filled his voice. "It appears his wing is broken."

The wing was bent, and not wanting to startle the bird, Daniel kept his distance, but he swore he could see a visible fracture.

"Poor sweet thing." Sympathy filled Jenna's voice. "I wonder if there is a wildlife rescue/rehabilitation agency in GraceTown."

She looked to Daniel as if expecting him to have the answer.

He pulled out his phone. "I don't know, but I can look up—"

"Not necessary." Violet stepped past him and Jenna. Bending over, she scooped up the bird and cupped him in her hands. The bird remained still, its beady eyes fixed on Violet.

"Don't be scared," Violet whispered to the bird. Time seemed to stretch until, finally, Violet opened her hands, and the oriole launched himself into the air.

Turning back to Jenna and Daniel, Violet smiled. "See? All better now."

Daniel exchanged a quick look with Jenna, then turned back to Violet. "His wing was broken."

Violet lifted her gaze to the sky, where the bird was now only a dark speck. "I don't think he could fly like that with a broken wing."

"But—"

Daniel didn't get a chance to say more.

"I believe this is my turnoff." Violet paused at the intersection and pointed.

"We can go with you," Jenna offered.

"That's okay." Violet smiled. "I want to look, you know, browse. It's better if I go alone. Besides, this way you can explore the town square and River Walk."

"If you're sure—"

"See you later." Without another word, Violet strode down the sidewalk away from them.

"Looks like you're stuck with me," Jenna quipped as she

watched her "sister" go. "The good news is now we don't have to speed-walk."

"That thing with the bird…" Daniel began.

"I'm so glad he's okay."

"He was injured, Jenna. His wing was broken." Daniel blew out a breath. "Then he was in her hands, and suddenly he was okay."

Jenna stopped walking and turned to him. "What are you saying? That Violet healed the bird?"

Daniel shoved his hands into his pockets and rocked back. "Looked that way to me."

"But that would be…" She hesitated, as if searching for the right word.

"Unexplainable? Supernatural?" Daniel met her incredulous gaze. "This town is known for such things."

"People keep saying that, but I don't get it. I mean, I haven't seen anything particularly unusual happen."

"You don't think Violet magically healing a bird qualifies as 'particularly unusual'?"

"We don't know that she healed the bird. Maybe his wing wasn't really broken. Last time I checked, you were a writer, not a veterinarian."

"Fair point. But you have to admit Violet is rather mysterious, isn't she? Maybe that's why she wanted to come to GraceTown. To reconnect with her magical roots."

"Okay, I think your writer's imagination is running a little wild."

Daniel shrugged. "Is it? I don't know. She seems to have no past. She has an uncanny sense about people. And—I can't stress this last point enough—she healed that bird."

Jenna stopped walking and put her hand on Daniel's arm. "Daniel, don't forget Violet was a foster kid. She doesn't necessarily *know* her past. Plus, kids in the system can get really good at reading people. It's survival." Then, worried she'd brought down the mood as they started to walk again, she added, "Or Violet is a magical being with healing powers."

Daniel nodded. "I'm just saying we should be open to all possibilities."

"You don't appear concerned about a supernatural teenager living in your midst."

"If healing an injured bird is her superpower, I don't think we have anything to worry about."

Jenna laughed. "Good point."

As they walked, Daniel noticed how the sunlight brought out the different shades of brown in her hair. "I don't know if you're aware, but the River Walk we'll be strolling down today is modeled after the one in San Antonio."

"That is so cool." Jenna looked up at him. "Thanks for asking me to walk. It would have been a shame to stay inside on such a nice night."

"I'm glad you said yes." Daniel liked seeing her relaxed and happy. He couldn't wait to stroll along the River Walk with her.

But the town square was now in sight, and it was beautiful, too. It looked much as he remembered, with the leafy trees even taller and the flowers along the walkway even brighter.

Still, his thoughts remained on their next destination. "When we get to the River Walk, I'll show you how my grandfather and I would go from one side of the creek to the other. We'd cross one bridge, walk a little farther and cross another back to the side we'd been on. Rinse and repeat. It was surprisingly entertaining."

"It might be fun to re-create that experience this evening."

Daniel returned her smile. He recalled that day so clearly. Like now, the sky had been a vivid blue, and the sun had been warm against their faces. His grandfather, a hat aficionado, had worn his favorite Panama. They'd laughed and talked and—

The feel of Jenna's fingers on his arm pulled Daniel from his reverie. His gaze shot to her.

"It's a gift, having such wonderful memories of someone you loved."

Before he could respond, a woman called Jenna's name.

Jenna whirled, then smiled broadly at the young woman who was rising from an ornate metal bench. A man, his hair as light as the woman's was dark, also pulled to his feet.

Both smiled welcomingly at Daniel. Did he know them? Neither looked familiar.

Then Jenna gestured with a hand toward the couple as they drew close. "Daniel, this is Sophie Wexman and her husband, Joe. Sophie owns the Timeless Treasures antique store. Joe is a professor at Collister College. He teaches…"

Jenna hesitated, as if trying to recall his field.

"Folklore studies." Joe extended his hand. "It's great to meet you. I read your first novel and liked it very much."

"Thank you." Daniel glanced at Jenna.

"I met Sophie at Timeless Treasures, and then she and Joe were at the party I attended the night you surprised me by coming to GraceTown," Jenna explained.

Daniel offered the couple a warm smile. "It's good to meet you both."

"I wish our paths had crossed earlier." Sophie glanced at her watch, then heaved a regretful sigh. "I'd love to stay and get better acquainted, but Joe and I are having dinner with my parents. We'll be late if we don't get going."

"Good to see you again, Jenna." Joe smiled. "Nice to meet you, Daniel."

When the couple strolled off—still holding hands—Daniel turned to Jenna to find out what else she knew about the couple, but she wasn't there.

He found her a few yards away, contemplating the angel statue.

"It's an amazing piece of art," Jenna murmured, almost to herself. "Her expression is so serene."

"I'm told it's a remarkable likeness of the woman who helped nurse the sick here during the 1918 flu pandemic."

Jenna shifted to face him, and surprise skittered across her face. "How would anyone know that?"

"On one of our trips to the square, Grandpa Fred gave me a history lesson." Daniel's lips curved ever so slightly. "It was so fascinating. I've never forgotten that conversation."

Daniel motioned with his head toward the bench that Sophie and her husband had just vacated. "Let's sit, and I'll tell you about it."

They sat, and after turning slightly to face each other, Daniel began the story. "This is about my great-grandfather William. He, along with several other civic leaders at the time, provided the funding for the statue."

Jenna offered an encouraging smile and patiently waited for him to continue.

"I don't know if you realize it—I certainly didn't—but the Spanish influenza outbreak had several waves, starting in 1918. Once the first wave was over, people were ready to get back to their normal lives."

"I can see that."

"William's friend Josiah warned him not to let down his guard, told him that a second wave was coming." Daniel's lips quirked upward. "Grandpa Fred said his father could be stubborn, and he didn't listen to his friend."

"Let me guess." Jenna tapped a finger against her lips. "William got influenza."

"Not him." Daniel expelled a breath. "His wife, Florence."

"Oh no."

"According to William, if this young woman depicted by the statue hadn't come into their home to nurse Florence, she would have died. Even with her care, it was apparently touch and go for a while."

"What was the woman's name?" Jenna asked.

"My grandfather couldn't remember. He wasn't even born at the time." Daniel blew out a breath. "He always said if it wasn't for the Angel of GraceTown, he wouldn't be here, and neither would I."

Jenna slowly nodded. "How many people did she end up helping?"

Daniel lifted his hands and let them drop. "No idea. Grandpa Fred only said that once a person was out of danger and recovering, she would move on to nurse the next. That went on until the pandemic had run its course."

"She never got sick?"

"That was the real miracle."

"Sophie thinks the angel looks like me." Jenna gave a little laugh.

Daniel studied the angel, then shifted his gaze back to Jenna. "I don't think the angel looks that much like you. I think it looks more like Violet."

"That's what I think, too." Jenna nodded emphatically. "I think it's a doppelgänger for Violet."

Daniel continued to study Jenna's features. "Yours and Violet's face are very similar, but yours is much more oval, and hers is slightly longer. Her smile is also different."

Puzzlement filled Jenna's eyes. "Her smile?"

"Yes, when she smiles, it's with only one side of her mouth, but when you smile, it spreads across your whole face."

"Wow. That's detailed."

Embarrassed, but not sure why, Daniel shoved his hands into his pockets. "Anyway, the statue looks like Violet."

"How did they come up with the face?"

Daniel blinked. "Pardon?"

"Who picked the face that would go on the statue? Was it the person who carved the statue?"

"From what I understand, the image came from William. He liked to draw, and while the young woman was in his house, caring for his wife, he sketched her." Daniel thought for a moment. "Now that I think about it, Grandpa Fred once showed me his sketches. I'm sure they're still somewhere in the house."

"I'd love to see them."

Daniel nodded. "Anyway, the story is that when several prominent men in the community decided to erect a statue in honor of the woman they'd begun calling the Angel of GraceTown, William gave the stonemason one of his sketches, and that's the face that's on there."

Jenna shook her head. "That's an amazing story."

"Do you think Violet could be related to that young woman?"

"I don't know enough of her background to say if that might be a possibility. Though, if you go far back enough in anyone's history, you can probably find a connection."

"What about you?"

"I don't have any family in this area, but like I said, go back far enough…" Jenna gestured. "C'mon, let's check out the River Walk while we talk."

She looked so pretty, standing there with the sun shining on her face. Her red lips reminded him of the strawberries in the garden.

He wondered if he kissed her if she'd taste as sweet as the berries. Or would such an action only damage the friendship they were building?

Smiling, Daniel settled for taking her hand. "Yes. Let's."

CHAPTER FOURTEEN

The next morning, Violet stopped short of the tall hedges surrounding the garden and turned to face Jenna, Daniel and Rosemary.

"You might not be aware, Daniel, but the garden area was a real mess when we arrived," she said. "Although the crew you hired did a stellar job mowing and trimming the rest of the lawn, this area—other than the hedge—was left to go to weed."

"The weeds were reproducing faster than a Catholic rabbit." Rosemary laughed at her own joke, then shook her head. "I can't recall ever seeing a more neglected garden."

Jenna nodded her agreement, glancing at Daniel. "It was really bad."

"I'm all about new life, about making things thrive." Violet met Daniel's gaze. "In terms of this garden, I proudly say, mission accomplished."

Rosemary opened the iron door leading to the garden, then stepped aside. "Prepare to be awed and amazed."

Jenna entered with Daniel right behind her and sucked in a breath. She'd been here before, but early on.

Rosemary was right. The sight before her both awed and amazed.

The weeds were history, and in their place, dark, rich soil sported an array of brightly colored flowers and plants with leaves that shimmered in the early morning light. On the other side of the garden, a variety of vegetable plants, most of which Jenna could not begin to identify, pushed out from the ground.

Her nose announced that herbs were here, too. The enticing aromas of lavender, mint and rosemary wafted in the air.

"It's like the Garden of Eden." Jenna breathed the words almost reverently.

"Not even close." Violet's blue eyes twinkled, then she turned to Daniel. "I believe your grandparents would be pleased to see this area returned to its former glory."

"They would." Daniel's gaze seemed to dart everywhere at once, as if he was trying to take it all in.

Jenna shook her head. "I can't believe the two of you did this all by yourselves."

"It was the craziest thing." Rosemary's voice held laughter. "I would plant something, and I'd say to Violet, 'I don't think this one is going to take.' Then I'd come out the next day and see Violet tending the plant, and it'd be thriving."

Shifting her gaze, Jenna shot Violet a questioning look.

The girl simply shrugged.

Daniel crouched down to rub a piece of lamb's ears between his fingers. He slowly stood, his expression puzzled. "My grandmother loved this plant. In fact, I remember hers being in this exact spot in the garden. How did you know?"

Violet smiled. "Everyone loves lamb's ears."

"Where did all the plants and fresh soil come from?" Jenna knew that even DIY landscaping didn't come cheap.

"Lennie, or maybe it was one of his lawn crew, told me about Leaves of Green's discard pile. Plants that are dead or nearly dead that you can get for super cheap." Violet smiled. "His lawn crew brought in the soil from another job where the people were digging a swimming pool and had extra dirt they wanted hauled away. Me taking it was doing him a favor."

"All these plants were half dead? How could they be flourishing like this after only a month? Even with new soil, I'd think—"

"Jenna." Violet's voice pulled Jenna's gaze away from the garden and back to the girl. "When things are where they're meant to be, they thrive."

Like we are. The thought entered Jenna's mind so clearly that, for a moment, she could have sworn Violet had also spoken the words aloud.

"Look at the bench." Delight filled Rosemary's voice as she pointed to the English garden bench big enough for three. "We found it in the carriage house."

Rosemary clasped her hands together, and her face took on a dreamy expression. "Now you and Daniel can sit and gaze out over your garden."

Jenna shook her head, keeping a smile on her lips. "Not my garden."

Daniel's garden. The clarification was on the tip of Jenna's tongue, but Daniel spoke first.

"The garden is all of ours." His eyes remained filled with wonder. "Thank you, Violet and Rosemary, for bringing this area back to life."

"Working the soil, planting and even the weeding was a labor of love." Pride filled Violet's eyes as she studied her masterpiece.

"Until I began working out here with Violet, I was convinced I had a black thumb." Rosemary chuckled.

Jenna thought of the poor spider plant back in Philadelphia. "No offense, my sweet aunt, but a couple months back, you couldn't grow mold on bread."

"That used to be true," Rosemary admitted with a rueful smile, "but here, all of a sudden, I'm a natural gardener."

"Rosemary has a love of life, and the plants sense that." Violet slung an arm around Rosemary's shoulders and gave a squeeze. "Plus, no one named Rosemary can be bad at gardening."

"Violet told me I just had to believe. I did, and look what happened." Rosemary smiled happily.

"Well, I'm impressed." Jenna couldn't think of anything else to say.

"Wait. Whoa. Is that a lemon tree?" Daniel's voice rose as he crossed to the other side of the garden.

Jenna strode with him to gaze disbelievingly at the tree and the yellow fruit hanging from its branches.

"They can be a bit difficult to grow," Violet acknowledged.

"Especially in this climate." Puzzlement furrowed his brow as he turned to Violet. "How'd you make that happen?"

Violet didn't immediately answer, then her head cocked, reminding Jenna of a hunting dog hearing a bird rustling in the bushes. "I believe Barry is at the front door."

A second later, the doorbell rang, the sound filtering through the kitchen's open window.

Rosemary smiled coquettishly. "He told me he might pop by this morning."

"I'm going inside with you." Violet looped an arm through Rosemary's and waved good-bye to Daniel and Jenna with her free hand. "You two take your time. Don't come back in too soon, or I'll think you were kidding when you said you love the changes."

Jenna watched Violet and Rosemary disappear into the house. When she turned, she found Daniel crouched beside the small tree, inspecting the lemons more closely.

He looked up at her, then straightened. "These kinds of trees aren't suited to Maryland's climate. I'm no expert, but I know you need a warm, sunny climate with mild winters for these to flourish outside."

"How did she get it to grow?" Jenna asked. "And the rest of the garden to be so robust?"

Daniel met her gaze. "How did she heal that bird?"

Jenna slowly shook her head. The possibilities that sprang to mind were too fantastical to voice. "I don't know."

Daniel nodded as if he understood, then gestured with his head to the bench. "Let's sit for a few."

They sat for several moments, each trying to make sense of the unexplainable while inhaling all the wonderful fragrances. As a minute ticked by, then two, Jenna focused on the tangible and what could be explained.

"I got up early this morning and looked for your grandfather's sketches," she told him. "The ones of the Angel of GraceTown."

Interest sparked in his green depths. "Any luck?"

"I found a couple of sketchbooks he filled during the war, but no sketches of the angel."

"Maybe they got tossed," Daniel suggested.

"I don't think so." Jenna gave a little laugh. "From what I've seen, your family kept just about everything."

"You're saying I come from a group of packrats?" he asked in a teasing tone.

"Only in the very best of ways." Jenna hesitated. "I know you're busy finishing up your book, but I was thinking…"

He offered an encouraging smile.

"One of these days, before you get started writing for the day, maybe you could come down and let me know what you'd like to keep and what can be tossed?"

"I can do that." He took her hand, gently lacing his fingers through hers. "In fact, it'll be my pleasure."

"How can you say that? You've seen the amount of stuff down there."

"The pleasure," he told her, "will be in spending time with you."

"We already spend a lot of time together."

"You know what I've discovered, Jenna?"

She shook her head, her gaze firmly fixed on his face, on those incredible green eyes.

"The more time I spend with you, the more time I want to spend with you."

There was a question in his eyes. Jenna knew she could ignore it, and Daniel would not press. But she wanted him to know how special this time with him was, wanted him to know that his interest wasn't one-sided.

Taking a deep breath, she took the leap. "It's the same for me."

She wrapped her arms around his neck, and the kiss came a heartbeat later, warm and full of promise.

Jenna embraced the moment, knowing that kissing Daniel with the sun shining down on them was something she would remember always.

That evening, Daniel strolled into the sitting area next to his bedroom and found Jenna curled up on the sofa with a book in her hand.

At the sound of his footsteps on the hardwood, she lifted her head. She sat straight up, running a hand through her tousled hair as she offered a smile. "Daniel. I didn't realize you use this room."

"I don't. Haven't." He dropped down on a nearby chair. "Until now."

"It's a beautiful space." Jenna gestured with one hand. "Elegant, but with a warm, homey feel."

"My grandparents spent as much time in this room as they did in the downstairs parlor." Glancing around the room, Daniel rested his gaze on the massive fireplace. "Grandpa Fred said that his grandfather, Richard Grace, had those art nouveau nature tiles specially made."

Following the direction of his gaze, Jenna smiled. "I like the birds."

"Not just any birds. Orioles. Like the one Violet rescued."

Jenna inclined her head. "Isn't the oriole the state bird of Maryland?"

"It is now, but back when the house was built and the tiles designed, it was simply a bird Richard admired because of its vivid colors."

"Well, for what it's worth, I think your great-great-grandfather made an excellent choice."

Daniel nodded his agreement and relaxed against the back of the chair. Conversation with her was exactly what he needed after hours at the computer. The only thing that would make this time more perfect? A glass of wine.

For the first time since he'd strolled into the room, Daniel settled his gaze on the open bottle of Merlot on the side table.

He gestured with his head. "Mind if I have some?"

"I'm happy to share, but I brought my glass and the bottle up from downstairs."

"Watch this." Daniel stood and crossed to a gorgeous burled wood cabinet against a far wall. With one strategically placed tap, the cabinet door swung open to reveal six cut crystal wineglasses and a T-model corkscrew in rosewood with a silver inlay.

"Ohmigosh, I didn't realize that section of the cabinet opened. I thought it was simply a decorative panel."

"Stick with me, kid." He grinned. "I know all sorts of secrets."

Jenna kept the smile on her lips. He could have his secrets. Just as long as she could keep hers...

"My grandparents liked to enjoy a glass of wine together in the evening."

"Those glasses are gorgeous, but they're bound to be dusty," Jenna warned.

Daniel held the glass up, and it caught the light.

"Not dusty at all." That fact led Daniel to make a mental note to increase Beverly's pay. The woman was thorough. After splashing some red wine into his glass, he resumed his seat in the chair. "What are you reading?"

Jenna held up the book. "*Anne of Green Gables*. I read it first as a girl and several times since. When I saw it in the bookcase downstairs, I brought it up here." For a second, worry skittered across her face. "I hope that's okay. It's an early edition, but I'm being extremely careful with it."

"I don't mind." Daniel gestured with one hand. "Mi casa es su casa. That goes for any of the books."

"Thank you." Setting the book aside, Jenna picked up her wineglass and sipped.

"My grandmother loved books, too. She was an avid reader and a fan of everything Lucy Maud Montgomery wrote." An image of his grandmother reading to him while he sat on her knee flashed before him. "She was the one who nurtured my love of the written word."

"How wonderful." Setting down her glass, Jenna gave him her full attention. "What kinds of books do you like to read?"

Daniel tapped a finger against his lips. He was an eclectic reader, and there were many books he admired. "Well, *The Great Gatsby*, for one. That book changed my life."

Surprise flared in Jenna's brown depths. "How did it change your life?"

"It made me want to be a writer. I read it when I was sixteen. After finishing it, I found myself wanting to someday create something that was that big and felt important."

"I know a lot of people like it, but I can't stand that book."

Daniel blinked. "Seriously? You don't like it?"

She gave her head a little shake. "Not at all."

"That is wrong," he blurted.

"Not wrong. Just my opinion." Her tone remained light as she took a sip of wine. "Opinions can't be right or wrong."

"Sure, they can," he immediately responded. "If you say, 'I admire that serial killer because he showed a lot of 'creativity,' that's a wrong opinion."

Jenna laughed. "Good point."

"I can't believe you don't like *Gatsby*. The whole world considers this a definitive work of American literature. It has an amazing legacy that I can only dream of as a writer. The iconic imagery, the rich descriptions, the complex characters."

Daniel had to stop himself before his commentary turned into a dissertation.

"If by 'complex,' you mean 'terrible,' then I agree with you." Jenna leaned forward, and her brown eyes flashed. "That book is a glorification of selfishness. Rich people who think the rules don't apply to them, people who feel justified in destroying whoever they want. From what I've read, even F. Scott Fitzgerald himself was more concerned with his own success than the health of his wife."

"Scott loved Zelda."

"Maybe. But did he care for her? Really care for her?" Jenna sat back and blew out a breath. "It's easy to love someone who is beautiful and fun and makes your life better. But when that person is hurting, are you willing to stop your fun to care for them?"

He opened his mouth, but shut it. It appeared Jenna was just getting warmed up.

"In my mind, love means loyalty, sticking by someone's side through good times and hard times." Jenna stopped abruptly and lifted a hand. "Sorry. As you can probably tell, selfishness is a hot button for me."

Daniel waited for several heartbeats, allowing the tension

pulsing in the room to dissipate. "I imagine you've seen that kind of behavior many times in your nursing career."

"Not all that often, but yes."

Daniel settled back in his chair. He had the feeling he was going to enjoy this discussion and, in the process, learn a little more about this captivating woman.

CHAPTER FIFTEEN

Taking a sip of wine, Jenna thought back. "I saw my share of challenging family dynamics."

While she *had* seen her fair share of those situations during her career, it wasn't any of those past patients who came to mind at this moment. It was Cherise and her husband. "The cases that were the most difficult for me to understand were ones where a couple appeared, on the surface, to have a good relationship. These were couples who'd enjoyed a vibrant social life and where one or both had successful, busy careers before their lives were upended by disease or injury."

"You had a ringside seat to what the people were truly like, deep down."

"Sadly, I discovered some were like Scott and Zelda. They put on a big public show, acting as if they truly cared, but when push came to shove, they didn't." Michael Menard had been like that, pretending he cherished Cherise, when all he really cherished was her money.

In the year she'd worked for the Menards, he'd spent less and less time with his wife while Parkinson's had stolen what was left of Cherise's independence. The exception, of course, was when he wanted her to loosen the purse strings. For years, her family's money had fueled their lavish lifestyle. Though Cherise's body was failing her, her mind remained sharp, and she kept a keen eye on expenditures.

"You mentioned seeing Gatsby as a wealthy person who thought the rules didn't apply to him." Daniel appeared to choose his words carefully. "Have you personally encountered anyone like that in your own life?"

Alarm bells began ringing in Jenna's head. The clamors didn't stop her from speaking honestly. "You know as well as I do that people like that are everywhere. They think their money and position give them the right to take advantage and destroy the lives of others."

Taking another sip of wine, Daniel rubbed his chin.

"Enough talk about *The Great Gatsby*." Jenna waved a dismissive hand as the calm that had wrapped around her like a favorite sweater slid to the floor and left her shivering.

"I agree," Daniel said with easy acquiescence. "No more *Gatsby*."

"Good."

"We'll talk Green Gables instead." Daniel gestured to the book she'd set aside. "For my grandmother, part of the lure of the series was the setting. She and my grandfather even once took a trip to Prince Edward Island."

"I'd love to go there someday," Jenna admitted with a wistful smile.

"What do you like most about the series?"

Jenna didn't have to think hard before answering. "The heartwarming theme of opening your heart to love. Of how the unexpected can lead to something wonderful and the importance of pursuing your dreams."

"Sounds like she packed a lot into the stories."

"You've never read them?" Why was she surprised? Jenna thought. The man loved Gatsby.

"I haven't," he admitted. "But hearing your passion for the stories makes me want to check out the series."

"The Green Gables books are comfort reads that leave me feeling good when I close the book." Jenna's lips curved. "I'm drawn to such stories. When I'm feeling stressed—as I have recently—reading something familiar and uplifting makes me feel better."

Concern blanketed Daniel's face. "I hope I haven't caused you any anxiety."

She offered a cheeky smile. "Not since you said we could stay."

That he had been so understanding still amazed her. That didn't mean she could quit worrying. The incident in Philadelphia still hung over her. But that wasn't something she could discuss. Not with him.

"Can I ask you a question?" she asked. "It's not related to our book discussion, but it's been nagging at me.".

He didn't even blink at the change in subject, merely took another sip of wine and gestured with his glass. "You can ask me anything."

"I saw how at ease you were with Ted and Anne. Even with Sophie and Joe. Why do you need us to run interference for you? You seem perfectly capable of handling any neighbors or old friends who cross your path."

"You mention feeling stressed. I've been feeling the same, and stress makes me shut down." Daniel's eyes took on a distant glow. "The thing is, since I've been here, my writing has been going well, and I've felt lighter and more like my old self than I have in years."

"I'm happy for you."

Daniel shot her a wink. "I also think being engaged to a beautiful woman agrees with me."

"Yeah, I'm sure that's what it is."

Her droll tone made him smile.

"I love New York, but it wasn't serving me anymore. I enjoy spending time with my friends who live there, and there's no shortage of things to do, but creatively I needed a change." Daniel spoke in a matter-of-fact tone. "GraceTown has been a good change."

Jenna thought about the changes she'd witnessed in other people since coming to GraceTown. Rosemary seemed sprightlier than she had in years. Violet, while always upbeat, seemed to fit with GraceTown in a way Jenna never would have expected. And Jenna, too, felt happier and more at peace than she had in, well, in longer than she could remember. And it wasn't lost on her that the handsome man sitting across from her was a big part of why.

When she noticed Daniel staring at her expectantly, she realized he'd asked her a question.

"I'm sorry. I spaced for a second. What did you say?"

Daniel laughed. "Glad to know I'm such interesting company!"

"Oh, no, I just—"

"Only teasing, Jenna. I asked if you think you'll return to Philadelphia. You know, after your sabbatical ends."

Jenna shrugged and offered Daniel a smile. "I guess it depends on whether the wind blows us in that direction."

Saturday morning dawned warm and sunny. Light streamed through the kitchen windows; the air fragrant with the scent of cinnamon on French toast.

"Who's up for a trip to check out the farmers market in the square this morning?" Rosemary gazed around the breakfast table. "I'd love some company."

Jenna thought of the boxes downstairs. Now that she knew a sketch of the Angel of GraceTown existed, or at least one had at one time, she was eager to start searching.

The hopeful look in Rosemary's eyes had her reconsidering. Hadn't she promised she would make those people who mattered to her a priority? If the sketch was in one of the boxes, it would still be there when she got back. "I'll go."

"Me, too." Violet flashed a smile.

Daniel set down his coffee cup. "Me, three."

Of all the responses, his surprised Jenna the most. She shifted in her seat. "I thought you were heading into the homestretch with your novel."

He shrugged. "We won't be gone all day. Besides, I've discovered getting out in the fresh air first thing in the morning clears my mind for work."

They left as soon as the table was cleared. Violet and Rosemary did their version of speed-walking, while Jenna and Daniel lagged behind them.

They could hear the bustle in the square when they were still blocks away. When it came into view, Jenna blinked. The area reminded her of a busy beehive. Not only were there dozens of vendor booths, the lovely spring weather had brought shoppers out in droves.

Pulling her gaze from the sea of bodies, Jenna slanted a sideways glance at Daniel. "Seeing this makes me glad we walked. I don't think we'd have been able to find a parking space within four or five blocks."

"Rosemary."

Jenna turned to see Barry, sporting a freshly trimmed Van Dyke beard, weaving his way through the crowd to stop at her aunt's side.

"This is a lovely surprise." Rosemary smiled in delight and grasped his hands, giving them a squeeze.

"A very nice surprise," he agreed.

Barry gazed at her aunt as if she was the prettiest woman—heck, the only woman—in the square. Jenna could see why he was smitten. Wearing a royal blue shirt that made her eyes look extra blue, her hair loose except for the hair pulled back from her face with a band, Rosemary definitely drew the eye.

Rosemary, engrossed in her conversation with Barry, didn't appear to notice them taking a step back to give her and Barry a little privacy.

"She looks so happy." Jenna spoke in a low voice meant for Daniel's and Violet's ears only.

"She is happy," Violet agreed. "Rosemary has blossomed here. She's built a community in a short period of time."

"Text me when you're on your way," Jenna heard Rosemary say. "My family and I have some shopping to do, but we should be home by then."

Barry shifted his attention to them, as if he was suddenly aware that Rosemary wasn't there alone. "It's nice to see you all here this morning."

"It's good to see you again, Barry." Jenna inclined her head. "What are you shopping for this morning?"

"Actually, I'm on the event committee that oversees the farmers' markets every year. This morning, I'm a troubleshooter."

Jenna smiled. "Sounds important."

"Not really." Barry chuckled good-naturedly. "It basically means walking about and taking care of any vendor issues and listening to what the shoppers have to say." Pride filled Barry's eyes as his gaze swept the square. "What do you think so far?"

"It looks great. So many interesting vendors. I can see why it's so packed."

"We like to think there is something for everyone." Barry smiled, then bent down to give a quick pat to a black-and-white Shih Tzu sporting a red bow strolling by on a leash. "Including items for our furry friends."

Barry turned back to Rosemary. "Is there anything in particular you're looking for that I can help you find?"

Rosemary gave his arm a pat. "Thank you, but we're just going to browse."

His gaze locked with hers. "I'll text you."

"I'm counting on it."

Her aunt's reply had Barry sauntering away, whistling.

Feeling a surge of excitement, Jenna reached over and squeezed Daniel's hand. "I'm so glad we came. This is going to be fun."

When Daniel wrapped his hand around hers and loosely linked their fingers, Jenna's heart skipped a beat.

Several minutes later, after buying a reusable shopping bag for their purchases, Daniel stopped in front of a stand selling asparagus. He glanced at Jenna. "I love asparagus, but I have no idea which stalks are the best."

"Firm, bright green stems."

Daniel turned to his right as a woman rolled up in a wheelchair. She was about his mother's age, with dark hair and quiet brown eyes.

"Lisa," Rosemary exclaimed, then bent over and gave the woman a hug. I didn't think I'd see you until next week."

"What's next week?" Jenna asked, stepping into the conversation.

"Card party." Rosemary and Lisa spoke at the same time, then laughed.

"Are you folks interested in asparagus?"

The woman manning the booth was polite, but her tone said if they weren't here to buy, they should move on and make room for real customers.

Leaning forward, Lisa picked up a handful of shoots and passed them to Daniel. "I don't know how many you want, but these are really nice. The stalks are straight, they have a smooth unwrinkled texture, and they're all about the same size."

"Why is the same size important?" Daniel asked.

"Similarly sized stalks help each stem cook evenly," Lisa explained.

"Thanks for the tip." Daniel extended his hand to Lisa. "I don't believe we've met. I'm Daniel Grace."

"Lisa Rogan, Beverly and Geraldine's neighbor. I know your name and your work, of course, but it's nice to meet you in person."

Once Daniel paid for the asparagus, they said their good-byes to Lisa.

"I'm going to check out that booth over there." Rosemary gestured to one selling jewelry. "I've heard they have some fabulous turquoise pieces."

"Is that Margaret?" Jenna asked, spotting Rosemary's friend holding up a turquoise and silver necklace.

Rosemary's smile widened in delight. "Well, so it is."

Jenna shook her head. "You're seeing everyone you know today."

"I'm lovin' it, too." Rosemary wiggled her fingers. "I'll catch up with you in a bit."

Jenna realized suddenly it was now just her and Daniel. She glanced around. "Where did Violet go?"

"She's over by the berries." Daniel gestured with one hand toward a large booth advertising, "Berries, Berries, Berries."

They walked over to find Violet deep in conversation with the berries vendor.

"Normally," the woman told Violet, "I have a lot more berries. This year, the plants just didn't produce as they have in the past."

"I wouldn't worry about it." Violet's strong tone rang with reassurance. "Next year will be far better."

"You sound very confident."

"I am." Violet smiled at the woman. "Wait and see."

Daniel glanced at Jenna. "You've got to admire her confidence."

Jenna nodded. "She's often confident about the future."

"Do you think," Daniel hesitated for half a heartbeat, "she *knows*?"

Jenna knew what he was asking. A week ago, she would have immediately dismissed the suggestion that Violet might have some kind of superpower.

"I'm not certain." Jenna met Daniel's gaze. "But at this moment, I'm leaning heavily toward maybe."

CHAPTER SIXTEEN

As soon as they arrived home, Violet headed to the garden, while Rosemary went upstairs to change for her date with Barry. Apparently, the man's civic duties were over at noon, and he planned to take Rosemary "somewhere nice" for lunch. The text from him saying he was on his way had arrived when they were climbing the porch steps.

The handles of the bag slung over his shoulder, Daniel followed Jenna into the kitchen to put away the asparagus, berries and snap peas.

Several minutes later, the sound of an engine as a car pulled into the driveway, followed by the screen door opening, had Daniel turning toward the front of the house.

"There are leftovers in the refrigerator if you get hungry," Rosemary called out just before the screen door banged shut.

Jenna chuckled and shook her head. "Sometimes it feels as if she's the one taking care of me."

Daniel smiled. "Knowing Rosemary, I'm betting the two of you always take care of each other."

"I believe you're right." Jenna stared at the bag of snap peas in her hand. "She's certainly doing a good job of reminding me that there is more to life than work."

"A happy life is a well-rounded one?"

"Something like that." Jenna's gaze grew distant, and he could see she was looking back. "The life I had in Philadelphia wasn't the life I wanted, but at the time, I couldn't see a way out."

Safe, he suddenly recalled. She had needed to find somewhere *safe*.

"I forget." He kept his tone casual and offhand. "What made you decide to take your sabbatical now?"

"My part-time position was eliminated." She spoke almost to herself. "Right after that was when everything fell apart—"

Jenna stopped abruptly. After waiting several seconds, he gently prompted, "What happened?"

She looked at him then, her eyes clear, but her expression still tentative. "You know that old saying about how when one door closes, God opens a window down the hall?"

Vaguely recalling a similar saying, Daniel nodded.

Jenna's lips curved. "Let's just say that GraceTown was my window."

Jenna didn't like keeping secrets, especially from Daniel, but she could see no other way to keep herself out of jail and Rosemary taken care of. Ensuring her aunt had what she needed to have a good life had to remain her priority.

After making a quick lunch, Daniel went upstairs to write, and Jenna took the wooden steps to the basement.

She paused at the base of the stairs. The cobwebs were gone, sucked away by a vacuum early on. The concrete floor had been mopped, and all the furniture had been moved to one section of the basement, organized by type.

One of these days, Daniel would come down and tell her if he wanted to keep all the furniture, or if there were pieces he wanted to sell. For now, they were fine where they were.

Her focus today was on the numerous boxes filled with correspondence, newspaper clippings and pictures. Grandpa Fred might have been a wonderful man, but organizing these items had obviously been a low priority.

Unless, Jenna thought, as she pulled out a yellowed newspaper clipping of his wife's obituary, going through these items would have brought him too many sad memories.

Jenna caught sight of the bare ring finger on her left hand. What would it be like to spend thirty, forty, fifty years with a spouse and then lose them? Jenna experienced a surge of sympathy for Fred.

Setting the obituary and newspaper clippings aside, she focused on several more canvas-bound sketchbooks of Daniel's great-grandfather's time as a soldier in the Great War. William had done sketches of French towns showing nothing but rubble, dead soldiers and cannons.

A heavy weight settled over Jenna as she thought about all that William and his fellow soldiers had seen, only to return home to face an even more deadly foe—Spanish influenza.

Each time she opened another sketchbook, she hoped to see a sketch of the Angel of GraceTown. All she found were more sketches showing death and destruction.

By the time she finished going through the fourth book, she needed a break from images of war. She shifted her attention to the boxes. She found some clear keepers in them, while other items she set aside to get Daniel's thoughts.

Footsteps on the stairs had her pushing back her chair and standing, taking a moment to stretch.

"Jenna, where are you?" Rosemary called.

"Keep walking. I've set up a work station just past the furniture."

"You've really got things looking good down here." Rosemary

stopped, then stared at the tabletop strewn with items from the past. "Oh my."

"I am making progress." Jenna chuckled. "Though it might not look like it."

"Is there anything I can do to help?"

For the first time, Jenna noticed that Rosemary was wearing a dress—not just any dress, but one of the two she usually reserved for special occasions. Covered with small flowers on a cream background, the dress flattered her coloring.

"You look lovely." Jenna gestured to a chair on the other side of the spare dining room table. "Sit and tell me all about lunch."

Rosemary pulled out the chair and sat, practically vibrating with excitement. "Oh, Jenna, Barry is such a dear man. We have so much in common. We talked and talked and talked some more."

"That's wonderful." It warmed Jenna's heart to see Rosemary so excited. "Do you think you'll be seeing him again?"

"I'm going over to his place next Friday for a family potluck." Clasping her hands together, Rosemary brought them to her bosom. "A number of his relatives will be there, and Barry is eager for me to get to know them."

"What are you going to take?"

"I don't know." Giddy with happiness, Rosemary gave a little laugh. "I'll figure out something. Oh, Jenna, I keep thinking if you hadn't decided to indulge my desire for a road trip, and if we hadn't picked up Violet, I never would have met Barry."

"Meant to be," Jenna said lightly.

"Just like you and Daniel."

Jenna smiled, because that's what she knew Rosemary expected. Her great-aunt had no idea that Jenna's situation was so dire.

She'd searched for more information on the jewel theft and eventually discovered a link to a post on a local news site that said the police suspected an employee, but that was it.

If the theft was really a big deal, surely there would be more media coverage. And wouldn't it have to be a big deal for the news to make it all the way to Maryland? So far, it hadn't.

Then again, the lack of coverage didn't mean the police along the Eastern Seaboard hadn't been notified.

Jenna wished—for not the first time—that there were more miles between here and Philadelphia. If she was smart, she would leave this place tomorrow. But could she really ask Rosemary to leave when she was so happy? When she was putting down roots and building her village?

No, Jenna thought, she couldn't do that to her aunt.

When she left, she would have to go alone. For a second, she considered the possibility that Violet might go with her, but then she reminded herself that GraceTown had been Violet's destination.

Daniel would do his best to look out for Violet and Rosemary. He had promised her.

Knowing that those she loved would be happy together would have to be enough.

～

Daniel glanced across the table at Jenna. "Thanks for coming with me tonight."

"You had me at 'Battle of the Bands.'" It wasn't exactly true, but Jenna had to admit that it had been an extra incentive to leave the house on a Saturday night.

"You know what that means, don't you?" He smiled at her, a teasing glint in his green eyes.

"That I need to get out more?"

He grinned and grasped her hand that lay on the tabletop. Then he surprised her by bringing it to his lips and planting a kiss on the knuckles. "That *we* need to get out more."

"You're probably right."

"No 'probably' about it," he said with a cheeky grin.

Jenna casually pulled her hand back. "Rosemary and Violet didn't seem to mind us missing the movie marathon."

In fact, Jenna thought, the two had practically pushed them out the door.

"Think about it." Daniel chuckled. "You can't veg out in front of the TV all night eating junk food with a nurse around. Too much of a reminder of how unhealthy you're being."

"You're saying I'm a buzzkill?" Jenna smiled.

"Yes."

"Hey!"

Daniel raised his hands in surrender. "To them! Not to me. To me, you're a delight." He shot Jenna his most charming smile, and she couldn't stop her laughter.

"I am a delight. And so is this place. How did you hear about it?" Jenna glanced around the bar. The Thirsty Pug sat just off the River Walk. She realized now it was lucky they'd come early to eat.

As the clock inched closer to eight, when the bands would perform, the tables as well as the stools at the bar had filled up. Now, it was standing room only.

"I ran across a childhood friend at the farmers' market this morning when you were picking out the snap peas. I asked for suggestions on things to do on a Saturday night. He mentioned a concert at the GraceTown Events Center, a performance of a Sherlock Holmes mystery onstage at Collister College and—"

"A Battle of the Bands at the Thirsty Pug," Jenna finished for him.

Daniel gazed at her with laughing eyes. "Since the concert and play are sold out, this seemed the obvious choice."

"Can I get either of you anything else?" Ainsley, a college-aged woman with pink hair and a nose ring, scooped up the empty red baskets that had once contained fish and chips.

Daniel looked at Jenna. She gave her head a little shake. She still had beer left in her glass.

"I'll take another draft," Daniel told Ainsley.

Since they would be walking home—unless they decided to grab an Uber—neither of them had to be the DD.

Ainsley flashed a smile. "Coming right up."

Ordering now appeared to have been the right move, because as soon as Ainsley returned with a pilsner glass of beer, the first band, aptly called Get Loud, took the stage.

In minutes, everyone in the bar was on their feet, including Jenna and Daniel. Unlike most in the audience, they didn't know all the words, but the catchy refrain came easily.

She smiled when Daniel slung an arm around her shoulders as they swayed and lifted their glasses of beer toward the ceiling with the rest of the crowd.

By the time their set ended, they were both smiling and thirsty from singing at the top of their lungs.

"They might as well give them the prize." Jenna took a sip of Daniel's beer. Her glass was empty now, and Ainsley was nowhere in sight.

Daniel smiled and lazily studied her. "Have I told you how beautiful you look tonight?"

"You may have mentioned that once or twice, but I don't mind hearing it again." Jenna shivered, recalling the look in his eyes when she'd come down the stairs and found him waiting.

He'd told her she looked beautiful and that he liked her bright yellow dress. That's when she'd confided that the skirt would flare out when she twirled. Of course he'd wanted a demonstration.

Despite telling him that was a one-time twirl and wouldn't be repeated, Jenna knew she'd give him another demonstration if he asked. Especially if he pulled her into his arms and kissed her like he had the first time.

"Looks like the second competitor is getting ready." Daniel

gestured with one hand, drawing her attention to where the band, Lonely Harry, was taking the stage.

While the band members tuned up, Jenna leaned into Daniel. Inhaling the delicious citrusy scent of his cologne had her momentarily forgetting what she'd been about to say. Until a couple of high-pitched giggles reached her ears. She pointed. "Do you think that's Lonely Harry?"

A man who looked like a lead singer, with a mop of brown hair cut short on the sides and messy on top, was surrounded by an adoring group of women, all of whom appeared to be in their early to midtwenties.

Daniel's lips quirked upward. "If it is, he doesn't look very lonely to me."

Jenna laughed, then gazed at Daniel through lowered lashes. "He's attractive, but not nearly as attractive as—"

She stopped. Had she really been about to say, *not nearly as attractive as you*? How could she be worse at flirting than her great-aunt?

"I feel the same about you." With great tenderness, Daniel tucked a strand of hair behind her ear, then brushed a kiss across her cheek.

At the touch of his lips, she felt her insecurity subside. How, Jenna wondered, could such a simple gesture have her heart swelling and desire surging?

Suddenly, Jenna wanted nothing more than to wrap her arms around his neck and kiss him until she was drunk on the taste of him. She wanted to hold him close and never let go. She wanted—

Lonely Harry launched into the first song of their set, and suddenly she was back on her feet.

This band was good, she admitted, after they'd finished the second of the three songs they would play. Get Loud still had her vote, though.

Lonely Harry's third song, a ballad, tugged at her heartstrings and brought tears to her eyes.

The last note lingered in the air before the crowd erupted into thunderous applause.

The song had been about a breakup, and the refrain—"never going to stop missing you"—struck at the heart of Jenna's fears.

She knew that was how it would be for her once she left GraceTown and Daniel. The knowledge that that time wasn't far off made the pain even more pronounced.

Unless... Did it have to be? What if she told Daniel the whole truth? He'd have no reason not to trust her. Unless you counted the fact that she had more or less broken into his house and lied about her identity to everyone he knew in town.

Stop it, Jenna, you're being silly. Daniel wouldn't see it that way. Yes, she'd been keeping secrets, but surely he would—

"Danny."

Daniel must have recognized the man's voice coming from behind them, because a smile was already on his lips when he turned in his seat.

"I'm glad you decided to take my suggestion and check out the place."

Jenna swiveled, and her heart stopped when she saw the uniformed police officer, his curious gaze focused on her.

Though Jenna's expression gave nothing away, Daniel felt her sudden tension because the fingers of her left hand were still laced with his.

"Logan." Daniel smiled at his childhood friend. "What are you doing in uniform?"

"I'm working tonight." Logan shrugged. "My partner and I are doing spot checks of the businesses in the area, making sure everyone is behaving themselves."

"How long have you been on the force?"

"Eight years now." Logan cast a curious glance in Jenna's direction. "Is this the fiancée everyone's talking about?"

"Hi." Jenna stuck out her hand. "I'm Jenna."

Daniel noticed Logan pause, as if waiting for Jenna to say more. When she didn't, Logan replied, "Logan Mattson. Pleased to meet you."

"Same. You two probably want to catch up. Why don't I grab you both something from the bar?"

"No, thank you. I'm working, so no drinks for me."

"A bottle of water, then?"

Daniel watched Jenna. Was it his imagination, or did she seem suddenly tense, despite her bright smile? She might even seem eager to get away.

"Please don't trouble yourself," Logan insisted, his voice friendly but firm. "I heard Danny had a girlfriend in New York. Didn't realize you'd decided to take the plunge and get married. How long have you been—"

Applause drowned out the rest of his question.

Logan's radio cackled, and he stepped away momentarily to answer. "I best get going," he said when he returned. "It was nice meeting you."

"Nice meeting you, too," Jenna called out.

Daniel leaned close to her ear. "Saved by the band."

The bright smile she'd had for Logan froze. "I don't understand what you mean."

"I think you do." Daniel met her gaze. "One of these days, I hope you'll trust me enough to tell me what it is you're running from."

CHAPTER SEVENTEEN

Sunday dawned with rain and cloudy skies. After breakfast, Daniel announced he was heading upstairs to write. Once she finished her coffee, Jenna planned to spend the day in the basement, organizing papers and searching for more sketchbooks.

Rosemary had gone to church with Barry and wasn't expected back until after lunch. Violet had slept in. She wandered into the kitchen in search of coffee and food—no doubt in that order—just as a chime sounded on Jenna's phone, alerting her that one of her Google Alerts had been triggered.

For a second, Jenna simply sat there, dread coursing up her spine. She told herself she was being silly. More than likely, the alert was simply another false alarm. For weeks, there had been few news articles about Michael Menard, none of which had pertained to her situation.

Out of the corner of her eye, Jenna caught Violet gazing at her with unabashed interest.

After several seconds had passed, Violet arched a brow. "Aren't you going to check it out?"

"I suppose." With a show of nonchalance, Jenna slipped the phone from her pocket and opened the article from the *Inquirer*.

Jenna quickly read the news item, avoiding looking at the campaign photo of the smiling man. Michael Menard, current city councilmember, had confirmed he planned to run for mayor of Philadelphia. It was the information further down in the article, about the police continuing to investigate a jewel theft in the Menard home, that had her breath hitching. The unnamed suspect, wanted for questioning, was reported to have been an employee in the Menard household.

Jenna's palms grew damp even as her thumbs flew across the phone screen as she searched for other articles that referenced the theft. She found none.

"Jenna."

Pulling her gaze from the phone, Jenna looked up.

"Take a couple of deep breaths and calm yourself." Violet's dulcet tone soothed like balm on a raw burn. "It will be okay."

"I-I'm fine." Rattled, Jenna stumbled over the words.

"The news about the theft is only in the Philadelphia papers." Violet spoke calmly, her expression serene, her warm blue eyes never leaving Jenna's face.

Jenna cleared her throat. "Are you saying you think I'm still safe here?"

Violet smiled and placed a hand on Jenna's arm, the gesture bringing comfort and the same sense of energy that Jenna had experienced before. "I'm saying you don't need to worry."

Not now maybe, Jenna thought, but the police clearly wanted to speak with her. Which meant Michael Menard had blamed her for the theft. She realized now that, down deep, she'd hoped his threat had been only bluster. She should have known better.

Michael Menard was a man who believed he was entitled to anything and everything he wanted. And, in his eyes, for someone like her—a mere employee in his household—to challenge that was an offense that demanded retaliation.

Jenna would have to leave GraceTown. She'd always known

she couldn't stay here—couldn't stay in any one place—for too long, but this news brought that outcome into sharp focus.

If the news had not spread beyond Philadelphia, then she had time to tie up loose ends here and figure out her next steps. Not much time. But some.

Violet's gaze searched hers. "Are you feeling better?"

"Steadier," Jenna admitted. "I'm going downstairs. I want to have everything organized before I…" She paused, then changed tacks. "I want you to be happy, Violet."

"I know you do." Violet met Jenna's gaze. "Just remember your happiness matters, too. Especially to those of us who love you."

Jenna did her best to put the article out of her mind as she descended the steps into the basement. She'd been working for a few hours in her normal spot when she heard footsteps approaching.

When Daniel popped into view, she smiled. "Just the man I wanted to see."

"I like hearing that." His eyes darkened with pleasure at the sight of her. Returning her smile, he skirted the table.

Jenna was already on her feet, her heart squeezing tight. Over the past week, she and Daniel had developed a routine.

Once he finished his pages, he would join her in the basement for a couple of hours of work. They'd talk, laugh and even manage to make progress on all the sorting, too.

"Did you have a productive morning?" she asked.

"I did." He stepped close. "How about you?"

"I've made some headway." Giving in to temptation, Jenna leaned forward and kissed him on the mouth.

She intended it to be a brief "glad to see you, welcome to the basement" kiss. It quickly morphed into more.

Enfolding her in his arms, he kissed her until her knees went weak, and her heart galloped an erratic rhythm.

At the point where she thought she might tear off her own clothes—or his—Jenna reluctantly stepped back. She cleared her throat. "What say we get to work?"

"Sure. Unless you prefer to kiss some more?" His eyes sparkled with good humor and...something more.

Calming the desire that still surged like an awakened river through her veins, Jenna pointed to the second chair by the table, not trusting herself to speak.

Obligingly, Daniel sat. His eyes widened. Apparently, he'd noticed the stack of canvas-bound sketchbooks.

"You hit the mother lode." His gaze lifted from the books to her. "Where did you find these?"

"In one of the boxes." Jenna shook her head, still unable to believe her good fortune. "They were under a bunch of papers instead of being with the others."

"Having them all together in one box would be too easy." Daniel chuckled, a low, pleasant, rumbling sound.

"Exactly. Before you get started, I want to show you something." Jenna had used a scrap of paper to mark the place in the sketchbook she had been perusing. She opened the book to that spot. "Is this William's wife, Florence?"

Daniel leaned close and studied the image. "Any photographs I recall seeing were when she was older. This is her, but she's much younger here." He shifted his gaze to Jenna. "I wonder if this was when they were dating."

Jenna gestured to her favorite sketch. "Look at this one. She's sniffing a single rose. Maybe the rose is from him?"

"It could be." Daniel's gaze remained on the sketch. "There's something about the way he draws her that says, 'I love this woman.'"

Jenna nodded. "I think it shows she loves him as well. Or he hopes she does."

"What makes you think that?"

Jenna pointed, the tip of her finger, not quite touching the paper. "See her big, dreamy eyes and that slightly openmouthed smile? To me, that says surprise and joy."

"You know what says love to me?"

She shifted her attention to him.

"The fact that there are so many sketches of her." Daniel flipped one page and then another. "We see her with the flower, on the porch swing, talking with friends, even praying while in church."

"It had to have been devastating for him when Florence contracted influenza."

"Especially if he didn't listen to his friend's warning and instead assumed the pandemic was over."

Jenna looked up at Daniel. "She wouldn't have blamed him. Even at her sickest, she wouldn't want him to carry that guilt."

"How can you be sure?"

"She loved him. If these pictures are any indication, he loved her, and she loved him. When you have such deep feelings for another, you don't want them to suffer."

Daniel met her gaze. "I would never want you to suffer."

"Daniel, I..." If things were different, Jenna might have encouraged him to speak from the heart.

She might have done the same. Instead, she only smiled, picked up one of the sketchbooks and handed it to him. "Let me know if you find anything interesting."

Even as Daniel slowly went through each sketchbook, page by page, he kept one eye on Jenna. He loved the way she smelled, like the flowers in the garden, and the way her hair fell softly against her cheeks as she turned the pages.

He loved her.

When he'd returned to GraceTown, he hadn't expected to find love here. Then again, he hadn't expected to find three strangers living in his house.

Daniel was grateful he'd been ill when he'd arrived, or he might have tossed them out that very night. Heck, he might have even called the police.

By the time he'd recovered, he'd gotten to know them. He'd known they weren't out to trash his house or take advantage. They'd simply needed a safe place to stay.

But why?

That was the piece of the puzzle that niggled at him and kept him from declaring his love for her. Something—someone—had caused her to leave Philadelphia.

He thought she had shared enough details that he could likely do an online search and figure out the story. Up until now, he'd refrained, not because he wasn't curious, but because he wanted Jenna to trust him enough to tell him the whole story.

Daniel glanced down at a newspaper clipping stuck between the pages of the sketchbook. Carefully removing it, he felt his heartbeat quicken as he read.

Setting it down, he flipped though several pages of the sketchbook, but found no sketches of the Angel of GraceTown. "Jenna."

Something in his voice must have alerted her that he had found something special, because she immediately shifted her attention to him.

"You found William's angel sketches?" Her voice shook with excitement. "Show me."

"Not those, not yet, but I found an article from when the angel statue was dedicated." He handed her the clipping.

Jenna glanced down briefly, then back up at him. "Where did you find this?"

"Mixed in with the sketches of Florence."

Jenna leaned over to study the image of Florence with a hand resting on her stomach, a dreamy look on her face. "She looks pregnant in this picture. What's the date on the clipping?"

"July, 1929." Daniel glanced at Jenna, thought for a moment, then nodded. "That would fit, since Grandpa Fred's oldest brother was born in 1930. My grandfather was their last child, born in 1940."

"But the influenza pandemic ended in 1919. Why would they wait nearly ten years to have the statue made and erected?"

"I would say that deciding to do the statue, agreeing on what it should look like, finding the person to do it and raising the money would all take time." Daniel pointed to the article. "This was unveiled in 1929, which says someone had been hard at work on it for a while."

"It might not have happened if they'd waited another year or so." Jenna stared thoughtfully at the date.

"How do you figure?"

"Didn't the stock market crash the fall of that year?" Jenna met his gaze. "People were flush with money in the 1920s, but that ended in October 1929."

Daniel rubbed his chin. "It would be so much easier if he'd dated these sketchbooks."

"Probably didn't even occur to him." Jenna shrugged. "These were simply books of his doodles."

After scanning the article, Daniel nodded. "This confirms what we thought. That money was gathered from those who the young woman helped. It appears these people came from all walks of life, but several wealthy benefactors covered the bulk of the cost."

Jenna gazed at the faded image of the statue and shook her head. "I still can't believe how much the face of that statue looks like Violet."

"And like you," he reminded her, then quickly added, "but definitely more like Violet."

"Violet is much more of the angel-type than me." Jenna stilled as a thought struck her. Violet couldn't be…could she?

Daniel's gaze met hers, and she could see his thoughts had veered in that same direction.

"Sometimes when Violet speaks to me or touches me, I get this odd sensation." Jenna tilted her head questioningly.

"That's happened to me, too," Daniel admitted.

"It's makes me wonder…" she began. "I mean, it's crazy to think that…"

"Completely crazy," he quickly agreed before she could complete the suspicion. "I know I joked about her healing the bird, but Violet actually being a hundred-year-old woman with magical powers is hard to believe—even in GraceTown."

Jenna expelled the breath she hadn't realized she'd been holding. "I think it's time we stop speculating and get back to work."

∼

Rosemary arched a brow. "You're seriously telling us you would rather sit down here and watch a movie you've seen a thousand times than, say, go upstairs and chat with your handsome fiancé?"

Her gaze shifting from Rosemary to Jenna, Violet popped a kernel of popcorn into her mouth from the bowl in her lap. "Doesn't make any sense to me. Especially since we all know how much you like your fiancé."

"Keep your voices down. He might hear you." Jenna wasn't sure what had gotten into her aunt and Violet. "And he's not my fiancé."

"He won't be for much longer with that attitude," Violet pointed out.

Jenna forced herself not to take the bait, reminding herself they were simply doing what they did best—teasing her. "I do not have an attitude, and I'm not trying to make Daniel into anything more than my friend."

"Fine, fine." Violet waved an airy hand. "Hot, talented writers who show kindness and compassion to you and your family aren't your type. Totally get it."

"You know what I mean," Jenna snapped back. Little sisters could be such a pain.

Rosemary brought a finger to her lips. "Something just occurred to me. Barry has a son. I could see if he's single."

"Har-har." Still, Jenna couldn't help but chuckle. "You two are terrible. Enjoy your movie. I'm going to bed."

"Now you're talking." Violet's comment had all three of them laughing.

"Good night." Jenna smiled all the way up the stairs.

When she saw the lights on in the sitting room, she gave a couple of sharp raps on the half-open door.

"Come in, Jenna."

Hearing the warm welcome in Daniel's voice had her smile widening as she stepped into the room and found him idly flipping through the book she'd finished reading just last night.

"I thought those were your footsteps I heard on the stairs." Smiling, he held up the book, *The Day That Changed Everything.* "This any good?"

Jenna moved to his side, took the book from his hand and dropped down on the sofa beside him. She realized almost immediately that she had misjudged the distance when she found herself practically on his lap.

"Sorry." Laughing, she scooted over, then shifted to face him.

"I don't mind." He shot her a wink. "You can sit on my lap anytime."

She returned his smile, and a languid warmth slid through her veins like warm honey. "Good to know."

Violet and Rosemary had been right. Being here with Daniel was so much better than watching a movie she'd seen a dozen times.

She dropped her gaze to the book in her hand. "Since you

prefer the classics and action-adventure books, I'm not sure if you'd like it, but I enjoyed it."

Curiosity glimmered in his emerald depths. "What did you like about it?"

"The story contained many of the themes I like."

Smiling, he motioned for her to continue when she didn't immediately elaborate. "C'mon, you can give me more than that."

Jenna brought the story into focus, then held up a hand and counted the points off on her fingers. "Resilience. Second chances. Starting over. The importance of forgiveness. The heart's capacity for love."

"Sounds like the author packed a lot into the story."

"Another part I liked was the focus on family, especially how people who are unrelated can come together to be a family."

A smile lifted the corners of Daniel's lips. "Like what the four of us have done."

Pleasure rippled through Jenna. That same thought had hit her as she'd read the book. "Yes, like us."

"What happened on the day everything fell apart?"

"You mean 'the day that changed everything.' So, at the beginning, her husband—"

"No." Daniel reached over and took her hand. "I'm not asking about the book. What happened?"

Jenna felt a pinching sensation in the area of her heart as she thought of how Daniel would feel when she simply took off one day. Would he understand she hadn't wanted to leave, but had seen no other way? "If I ever do something that ends up hurting you, I hope you'll understand that was never my intention."

CHAPTER EIGHTEEN

On Monday, after firing off a quick text to Calista to let her know his first draft was done, Daniel headed downstairs with a spring in his step. The story felt solid. Though Calista and her team would undoubtedly have suggestions and there would be rewriting, Daniel knew—he felt in his bones—that this book would be another winner.

When Daniel reached the bottom of the stairs, instead of hearing familiar voices coming from the kitchen, the laughter and sounds of female conversation appeared to come from the porch.

He stepped out to find not three women, but five. Beverly and Geraldine sat, holding coffee cups, while the other three had platters of food on their laps.

"Good morning, ladies." He let his gaze sweep the group, lingering on Jenna for an extra heartbeat.

Beverly must have noticed, because she waved a hand. "Go ahead and kiss your fiancée. We don't mind."

With all eyes on him, Daniel dutifully bent over. He hesitated for a second, giving Jenna a chance to offer her cheek, but she only smiled and lifted her face. He settled his mouth against hers for a brief, sweet kiss. "Good morning."

Jenna continued to gaze up at him through lowered lashes, a smile tugging at the corners of her lips. "Good morning back."

Daniel dropped down into the seat beside her and realized that the chair being available for him had been deliberate. They'd been expecting, or at least hoping, he'd join them. A warm rush of emotion slid through his veins.

"Do you have a wedding date set yet?" Beverly asked, her eyes bright with interest.

"No date yet," Violet answered, saving him the trouble of responding.

"You're going to make such a beautiful bride, Jenna." Beverly practically sighed the words. "Don't you think so, Daniel?"

Jenna, Daniel noted, carefully avoided looking in his direction.

His answer to this question came easily. "She definitely will."

"I'll get to your stuck window once I finish my coffee," Geraldine said, obviously done with the wedding talk. "If that works for you."

"That's fine."

From what Daniel had observed since arriving in GraceTown, Geraldine had mad skills. The woman was truly not only a jack-of-all-trades, but a master-of-all.

Rosemary, her hair pulled back into a single long braid down her back, gestured widely with one hand. "It's going to be a gorgeous day."

"It already is," Beverly agreed. "Lovely weather and scintillating conversation with friends. Life doesn't get much better."

Nods of agreement followed the woman's pronouncement.

"There's a piece of breakfast strata for you in the oven," Violet informed Daniel. "I substituted Gruyère for fontina, and it's very yummy."

That's right, Daniel thought, this was Violet's day to prepare meals. "Thanks for saving me a piece."

"You're welcome. We have plenty." Violet gestured with one hand in Beverly and Geraldine's direction. "I tried to give a piece to these two, but they'd already eaten."

"Let me get you the strata and some coffee." Rosemary started to rise.

"You sit." Daniel motioned her down. "I can get my own."

Instead of immediately heading for the kitchen, Daniel glanced around this collection of women who were the epitome of family.

He might not have been able to make his relationship with Calista work. He couldn't make his relationship with his family work. But in this little group, he fit.

Jenna, her lips as red as the tiny strawberries on her dress, pushed to her feet. "I'm going to put more coffee in the carafe. So, everyone drink up now. I'll refill your cups when I get back."

Daniel held the screen door open for her, catching the faint scent of vanilla as she stepped past him into the house.

He waited until they were nearly to the kitchen to give her the news. "I finished the book."

She whirled; her eyes wide. "All of it?"

"To the end." Daniel couldn't keep the pride from his voice. He'd finished other books before, but this one, well, this story had been a challenge. The fact that he hadn't given up, that he'd persevered, had pride surging.

Jenna set the carafe on the counter. Suddenly, her arms were around him, and she was hugging him. "Congratulations."

His arms wrapped around her, and for several seconds, he reveled in the closeness. "I'm definitely in the mood to celebrate."

Stepping back from his arms, she smiled up at him. "We could do a special family dinner?"

"I have this tradition."

Curiosity sparked in her brown eyes. "What kind of tradition?"

"When I finished my first book, I went to this fancy French café in New York, feasted on a meal of boeuf bourguignon and drank champagne." His gaze searched her face. "GraceTown might not have that exact place, but it's got some good restaurants."

"There seems to be an abundance of them." Jenna nodded. "I'm sure you can find one you like."

"I want you to come with me." Daniel took her hands in his. "I couldn't have finished the book without you. Your care when I was sick healed more than my flu. It somehow brought my creativity back."

"You give me too much credit."

"C'mon, Jenna, celebrate with me." Once again, he leaned forward and brushed her lips with his, lingering there for several heartbeats. "It won't be a celebration without you."

The next night, Jenna glanced down at the stretchy red wrap dress she'd just put on, then back at Violet. "I shouldn't be doing this."

"Doing what?" Violet sat cross-legged on the bed, gazing at Jenna with an inscrutable expression. "Enjoying dinner at a nice French restaurant with a guy you think is hot?"

"Keep pretending that there could be something lasting between me and Daniel." Jenna dropped down to sit on the bed beside Violet.

"You're just feeling guilty because you haven't yet told him the whole truth."

Violet remained uncannily accurate in reading her.

"He knows you're not my sister."

"I was the one who told him that forever ago," Violet pointed out. "Telling him what you're running from seems like a good next step."

"That isn't happening. Before he was a writer, he was an attorney, remember? Technically, he still is. He could, I don't know, get disbarred for harboring a fugitive." Jenna shook her head at her reflection. "I will not pull him into my mess."

"You appear determined to wage this battle alone." Violet studied her thoughtfully. "Trust him, Jenna."

"I'm not going it alone. You and Rosemary—"

"You won't lean on us, even if we want you to, even if you need us." Violet waved a dismissive hand.

"Violet, it's not that I don't appreciate your support or that I don't trust Daniel." Jenna turned to face Violet. "I do. But what I want more than anything is for all of you to be safe and happy. You deserve that."

"And so do you." Violet put her hands softly on Jenna's shoulder and turned her back toward the mirror. The women gazed at their reflection together. They truly did look like sisters. "I want you to savor every moment of this evening, Jenna. Don't worry about the future tonight, simply enjoy the here and now."

"I don't know…"

"You have no choice." Violet shot her a saucy smile. "You have to go."

At Jenna's arched brow, Violet continued. "Rosemary and I have plans for the evening. Plans that depend on you and Daniel being gone."

Jenna found herself intrigued. "What kind of plans?"

"A *Stars Wars* movie marathon."

Jenna made a face.

"That face is exactly why we're doing this when you're not here."

~

An hour later, sitting across the table from Daniel in Normandy, an upscale French restaurant, Jenna found herself taking Violet's advice and savoring the moment.

Daniel looked so yummy in his dark suit. He smelled every bit as good as he looked. One word described him tonight. *Irresistible.*

His eyes met hers and held. He smiled and lifted his flute of champagne. "To a beautiful night with a beautiful woman."

She clinked her flute against his. "I thought we were toasting to finishing the book."

Chuckling, he set down his glass. "That, too."

Daniel took a sip, his green eyes shimmering in the candle-light. "Actually, I have another bit of news to share."

"What kind of news?" Jenna sipped from her own flute.

"I've decided to settle in GraceTown permanently."

"Daniel, that's wonderful." Jenna reached across the linen-clad table and gave his hand a squeeze. "When did you decide this?"

"I've been thinking about it ever since I arrived. Well, once I started feeling better, that is." Daniel's gaze turned serious. "The three of you were right when you said a house shouldn't sit empty. This house is meant to be a home."

Jenna nodded, then smiled when the waiter placed the dishes they'd ordered in front of them, boeuf bourguignon for him and le saumon for her. "This looks lovely, thank you."

"May I get either of you anything else at this time?" the young man asked.

Daniel glanced at Jenna, who shook her head. "We're fine for now."

"I'll be checking back frequently. Please let me know if there is anything at all you need."

Jenna lifted her fork, but paused, her gaze fixed on Daniel. "I'm happy you're staying."

"Stay with me."

Jenna's salmon dropped back to her plate. Daniel hurried on before she could speak.

"I want you to stay. Rosemary and Violet, too." His gaze met hers. "Everyone is happy. I've felt more creative than I have in years. I can even help Violet with school. You can get a job nursing here, and we can have parties and take trips to New York. We'll get involved in the community and build a network of good friends, just like Rosemary has."

What Daniel was describing was a dream, the kind of life Jenna had always wanted but had never had.

Could still not have, she reminded herself.

Jenna broke from Daniel's gaze and dropped her eyes to her plate. The dish that had looked so beautiful moments ago suddenly seemed cold and heavy. She spoke without looking up. "We hadn't planned on staying this long. Yet, here we still are."

The light tone she'd tried for fell spectacularly flat.

"Because you know this is where you're meant to be." Daniel's tone rang with confidence. "I'm betting that Rosemary has no intention of leaving."

"You're probably right." Jenna scooped up some of the Parmesan risotto, but still couldn't look at Daniel. The asparagus that had been added to the risotto made her think of their shopping trip to the farmers' market.

She forced herself to breathe past the sudden tightness in her chest. Rosemary would insist on going with her if she left, but Jenna wouldn't take her away from her friends…and Barry. She would think of a way to make Rosemary believe she was doing Jenna a favor by staying.

"In the fall, Violet will likely be off at college." Daniel's lips curved as he took another bite of the beef braised in red wine, but his gaze remained steady on her face.

Finally, Jenna met his eyes. "I hope so."

In the end, Jenna knew that Violet would do as she pleased.

While she wasn't sure college was in the girl's future, it was kind of Daniel to make the offer to help her.

It didn't surprise her. Daniel was a kind man. A good man. The kind of man she could be happy with…under different circumstances.

"Daniel, you paint a lovely picture, but…I still haven't decided if I want to stay in GraceTown." Liar, liar, liar, the voice inside her screamed. She wanted to stay in GraceTown—stay with Daniel—with all her heart. But as soon as she'd seen that article in *The Philadelphia Inquirer*, she'd started making plans to leave.

"I don't understand why you'd still be contemplating leaving." Daniel's tone remained offhand, but his eyes were now sharp and assessing. "Don't you like it here?"

Not like it here? Who wouldn't like it here? If Jenna had had a choice, well, there was nowhere else she'd rather live.

You don't have a choice, she reminded herself.

"Jenna," he prompted, his voice as soft as the look in his eyes. "Don't you like it here?"

"I love it here." The admission popped out before she could pull it back.

His placid expression never changed. He inclined his head. "Is it me, then? You don't want to stay because of me?"

"How can you think that?" she cried. Didn't he know, couldn't he tell, how much he meant to her?

"Then why would you leave?"

Tell him. She could hear Violet's words. *Trust him.*

"Will you stop with all the questions?" The words shot out from between lips that suddenly felt frozen. "None of this can happen because you don't know me, not really."

"I think I do." He reached across the table for her hand, but she jerked it back.

"You don't."

"Then tell me."

Jenna pressed her lips and shook her head, not trusting herself to speak.

The excited, happy light in his eyes disappeared. "Is the problem that you don't trust me, or that you don't love me?"

Though everything in Jenna urged her to tell him the truth, the words wouldn't come. It was strange, really. The more she got to know and love him, the more she trusted him. At the same time, the more protective she became.

"Never mind." His expression was now that of a stranger. "No answer *is* an answer."

He pulled several large bills from his pocket and laid them on the table, along with his car keys. "I need to walk. I'll see you back at the house."

Not at *home*, Jenna thought, resisting the urge to weep. At the *house*.

She'd been living in a fantasyland the past couple of months, pretending she had friends, a man who loved her and a home. Just like every other place she'd ever lived, this wasn't a forever home, but simply a pitstop before she'd have to pack up and move on to somewhere else.

CHAPTER NINETEEN

Remembering Violet and Rosemary's movie marathon, Jenna didn't head back immediately. Instead, she sat in Daniel's car in the Normandy parking lot for what felt like hours, until she felt that even die-hard *Star Wars* fans like Violet and Rosemary would have called it a night.

When she walked through the front door, Violet informed her that Daniel wasn't home yet, and Rosemary had gone to bed.

While making the pronouncements, she had risen from the sofa and followed Jenna upstairs to her room.

Violet didn't ask what had happened. Jenna saw when the girl's gaze met hers that Violet knew everything that had gone on between her and Daniel this evening.

Several long seconds ticked by as Violet continued to study her with fathomless blue eyes. "I believe it's time you looked at what's really going on with you instead of hiding behind made-up fears."

Jenna bristled. "Violet, please, I'm too tired to—"

"We both know it's highly unlikely that your troubles will spill over onto any of us." Violet lifted a hand when Jenna opened her mouth to speak. "At the beginning, your concern for Rosemary's welfare had merit. She was isolated and totally dependent on you. That is no longer the case. She has friends here who love her and would support her. Me? I'm very capable of managing my own life."

"Daniel is an attorney—"

"He's also a well-known author with money and significant family connections. If there were to be an issue, he has the ability —and the desire—to help you, a fact he's already proven by letting us stay here."

Jenna could think of no response to what Violet was saying.

"Yet you hold back the truth with the excuse of protecting him. We both know that isn't the real reason you won't confide in him."

"I don't know what you're talking about."

"I think you do." The sympathy in Violet's eyes touched some-thing deep inside Jenna. "All your life, you've taken great care not to form deep attachments. From the time you were young, you taught yourself not to get too attached. Not to a place, to a school, to friends or even to boys you dated, because you knew you would eventually be forced to move away."

"Please stop trying to analyze me, Violet. You can't presume to know my life story." Though Jenna tried to sound firm, her voice wavered.

Because Violet was right, and they both knew it.

"Rosemary needed you, and you stepped up. I would venture to say you needed her just as much. She gave you a reason not to open your heart fully to anyone, because you had her and her needs to consider. You couldn't fall in love. You didn't have time to even date. Then along comes Daniel. He slides beneath those barriers you've erected. You've convinced yourself you're protecting him, when in truth, you're protecting your heart by refusing to share thoughts and fears that would deepen your connection."

"Violet, stop! You talk about being truthful," Jenna shot back, "but you were never a foster child, not really."

Violet smiled. "When you're trying to help someone who only wants to give help, never receive it, you have to get creative."

"Who are you? What are you?"

"I go wherever people need care, and I do what needs to be done." Violet's soft blue eyes darkened. "When I first came to Grace-Town, so many were sick. Nursing was the help they needed, so that's what I did. But I've been many things. A teacher, a farmer, a—"

"Foster child."

"Yes." Reaching out, Violet grasped Jenna's hand, and Jenna experienced the familiar surge of energy.

"You're wrong about me being scared to commit, Violet. I love Daniel, and I want nothing more than to spend the rest of my life with him."

Violet continued to stare expectantly at her.

"But I can't have a life with him, not the kind we both deserve, as long as this thing with Michael Menard is hanging over me."

"Well, there's your answer."

Jenna threw her hands in the air, and her voice rose despite her efforts to control it. "What answer?"

Violet's steady gaze never wavered. "That it's time to toss aside that spirit of fear, stop running and confront the situation head on."

Jenna doubted she'd gotten more than an hour or two of sleep. All night, she'd lain in bed, staring up at the ceiling, thinking of what Violet had said and trying to figure out next steps.

Violet clearly thought she should stay and fight. The thing was, Violet didn't know Michael Menard and the power he wielded in Philadelphia. His assistant, Mr. Spahr, was also well regarded. With him apparently willing to corroborate Mr. Menard's account of what had happened, what chance did Jenna have of convincing the police otherwise?

As she hadn't taken any jewels, the police wouldn't find them in her possession or any money on her from the sale of them. Of course, the district attorney would likely tell the jurors that she must have hidden them.

The prosecutor would likely paint her as someone barely getting by who'd seized on an opportunity to improve her circumstances. As far as the assault occurring when Mr. Menard allegedly caught her attempting to open the safe, that would be all too believable, especially with Mr. Spahr being a witness.

The only good to come out of this entire mess was Rosemary had found a place where she would be happy. Although her great-aunt had been a wanderer when she was young and wouldn't complain if Jenna insisted on them moving every couple of years, this time in GraceTown had shown Jenna the kind of life Rosemary needed and deserved.

Violet, well, did Jenna need to worry too much about a magical being?

That left only Daniel. The look in his eyes last night tore at her heart. She could only imagine how he would react when he found out she'd been lying to him all this time.

By the time dawn broke, Jenna concluded that her original instinct held—leaving was the right course of action. With eyes gritty from lack of sleep, she wrote letters to the three people who mattered most in her life.

She began with Violet and ended with Daniel.

As Rosemary and Daniel were completely in the dark regarding the events that had transpired in the Menard household, she went into detail in their letters on what had happened the day everything had changed.

Then she slipped the letters into envelopes. Her hand trembled as she carefully wrote each name across the front.

The art nouveau holder sitting on her dresser, the one she'd intended to give to Daniel but had yet to do so, caught her eye. When she was ready to leave, she would put the letters in it and place it in the sitting room between her bedroom and his.

She couldn't recall Daniel ever going into that area during the day. By the time he did wander in there this evening, she would be long gone.

For the best, she told herself.

Convinced this was the only course of action that made sense, Jenna straightened her shoulders and headed down the stairs for breakfast.

Daniel stood when Jenna entered the kitchen. His heart gave a lurch at her drawn face and tired eyes. She looked like she hadn't slept any better than he had.

Last night had been a major cluster, and for that, he deserved all the blame. He'd behaved horribly.

After storming out of Normandy, he'd paced the River Walk, using the walkways over the water to go from one side to the other, wishing his life now could be as uncomplicated as it had been when he'd been a boy and his grandfather had been all knowing.

He'd been so angry at Jenna that it had taken some time for him to realize just how badly he'd acted. Instead of discussing her reluctance to stay in GraceTown like a rational human being, he'd pushed her into a corner. When that hadn't achieved the desired response, he'd stalked away like a petulant sixteen-year-old.

Daniel still couldn't believe he'd walked out of the restaurant and left her to finish the meal alone. What kind of man did that?

He knew Jenna, knew she loved him, too, though neither of

them had spoken their feelings aloud. That love was why they would get through this.

At least that's what he'd been assuring himself until he'd come downstairs and found her seat at the table empty. Now that she had shown up and her gaze, distant and devoid of any emotion, landed on him, he suddenly wasn't so sure.

"Good morning, everyone." Jenna's spoke in a hearty tone at odds with her demeanor.

Because Daniel kept his eyes firmly fixed on Jenna, he sensed, rather than saw, Rosemary and Violet exchange glances.

Rosemary, who'd eaten only a couple bites of the oatmeal she'd just finished dousing with brown sugar, raisins and cream, abruptly stood. "Violet, could you please come with me to the garden? I want to show you the plant that Barry gave me yesterday and see where you think I should put it."

Jenna turned to her aunt, her brows furrowed in puzzlement. "Don't you want to eat your breakfast first?"

Violet rose. "This will just take a second."

Once the back screen door banged shut, Jenna expelled a heavy sigh.

"It's obvious this is a ruse to give you and me some alone time." Jenna poured herself a cup of coffee, but made no move to pick it up from the counter.

"Pretty transparent," he agreed with a smile.

"Sweet but misguided."

Daniel stepped to her then. "I owe you an apology."

Before the words had even made it out of his mouth, she was already shaking her head.

"Yes," he insisted. "I do. I should never have reacted the way I did, not when you were simply being honest with me. I never should have walked away from you like that. I am making a promise to you that it will never happen again."

"Really, Daniel, it's—"

"You matter so much to me." Taking a chance, he moved close

and opened his arms. When she stepped into them, he wrapped his arms around her, all the pent-up tension leaving his body. "I hate it that I hurt you."

"Sometimes it can't be helped," she said against his shirtfront.

"I acted badly." He would not take the out she was giving him. "I am sincerely sorry. Will you forgive me?"

She lifted her head, and when he saw the tears welling in her eyes, he felt even more like a louse.

"I am truly sorry…"

"It's okay. We all make mistakes." She expelled a long breath. "If you want my forgiveness, you've got it."

"I won't press you anymore about staying," he promised. "We'll just take things one day at a time. How does that sound?"

The return of Rosemary and Violet didn't give her time enough to answer, but the fact that Jenna had forgiven him buoyed Daniel's spirits.

"Did you two find a spot for the plant?" he asked Rosemary, feeling hungry for the first time since he'd stormed out of Normandy last night.

Rosemary beamed. "We did."

"We found the perfect place." Violet glanced at Jenna. "Sometimes you just know."

"Know what?" Jenna asked.

"Where something—or even someone—fits."

"Sometimes you're wrong, and it was never meant to be there at all." Shoulders now ramrod straight, Jenna snatched her coffee cup from the counter, her lips pressed together in a grim line.

Something going on here, Daniel thought. If he hadn't been so exhausted, he could easily figure it out. He was good with subtext.

"If you two don't fancy oatmeal, Violet and I whipped up cinnamon scones this morning," Rosemary told them. "We thought it'd be nice to enjoy a little sweet with the healthy."

"We need to hold off on the sweet," Violet told the older

woman, her expression turning watchful as her gaze shifted to the front door. "We have company."

Rosemary shot the girl a puzzled look. "Company? It's just the four of us."

The ringing of the doorbell had Rosemary's eyes widening. Then she chuckled. "I guess that's the company."

Jenna blanched.

"I'll get the door," Daniel said when no one made a move to answer.

He found himself equally puzzled. Who would be stopping by so early in the day?

The doorbell rang again, and Daniel covered the last few feet in several long strides. He didn't bother with the peep, always a good idea, but not a necessity in a town like GraceTown.

His eyes widened at the sight of the blond woman standing on the porch, looking as if she'd just left the office for a rendezvous at a martini bar in Midtown Manhattan.

"Calista, this is a surprise." Daniel stepped to the side. "Please, come in."

"I thought about calling and telling you I was coming," she told him, "but I didn't want to be put off. I—"

Calista paused as if only now realizing they weren't alone.

Her gaze shifted from him to the three women who'd apparently followed him into the parlor, then back to Daniel. "I didn't realize you had guests."

"We live here." Violet spoke in a friendly yet matter-of-fact tone. "You're his editor, Calista Evers." The girl held out a hand. "I'm Violet. It's a pleasure to meet you. Daniel speaks highly of you."

"Well, thank you." Calista glanced at Daniel.

"I'm Rosemary Woodsen, and this is my niece, Jenna." Rosemary stepped forward, all smiles. "Would you like a scone and some coffee? Made fresh this morning."

"I appreciate the offer, but I have some private business I need to discuss with Daniel." Calista, Daniel noted, paid particular attention to Jenna.

He could understand why. Jenna looked incredibly lovely in a simple summer dress covered in poppies.

"It's lovely to meet you, Ms. Evers." Jenna turned to Daniel. "We'll head back into the kitchen and give the two of you some privacy."

Once he was alone with Calista, Daniel gestured to the sofa.

Calista sat and crossed one long leg over the other. She glanced around the house. "When I drove up and saw this house, I immediately thought of your loft. From modern to vintage in one quick leap."

Daniel smiled. "Pretty much."

"This is lovely. My grandparents love these kinds of houses. Knowing you, I bet you can't wait to get back to the city."

"Actually, we all really like it here." Daniel thought of the pot of coffee in the kitchen. "Are you sure I can't get you a cup of coffee?"

"Nothing for me, thank you." Calista studied his face. "What's with the 'we'? Who are these women, Daniel?"

"They're my guests." Daniel knew that word did not convey the depth of his feelings for the threesome. Rosemary and Violet, well, they were family, and Jenna...

He couldn't stop the smile.

"Where are they from?"

"Philadelphia." Daniel wasn't surprised by the questions. Calista had a curious mind.

"Does Jenna work?"

"She's a nurse, but on sabbatical right now."

Calista's gaze turned sharp and assessing. "Is Jenna why you left the city to come here and write?"

To explain how it had all happened would take too much time, and it wasn't really any of Calista's business.

"Tell me why you made the trip here, Calista." Daniel kept his tone easy. "I emailed you on Monday that the book is nearly ready to send and promised you'd have it at the first of next week."

"That's what you said." Calista appeared to be choosing her words carefully. "You also said you'd gone in an unexpected direction, but gave no details."

"You're going to love it," Daniel assured her.

"I believe you. So why not let me read what you have?"

"Superstitious, maybe." Daniel shrugged. "The writing has been going well without any outside input. What if I give it to you before I review it, and then I'm stuck again?"

"You remember that my job is to help you when you're stuck?"

"And you are helping me by letting me do this the way I need to." Daniel smiled. "I want to go through it one more time, then it will definitely be in your inbox on Monday."

Calista's lips pressed together. "I don't know why you're being so obstinate."

"I don't understand why it's such a big deal for you to have it today, rather than next week."

Jenna appeared. "Sorry to disturb you. I'm heading upstairs. Again, it was nice to meet you, Ms. Evers."

"Lovely to meet you as well, Ms. Woodsen." Calista appeared to put extra emphasis on the *Ms. Woodsen*.

Daniel experienced a stirring of unease, though exactly why he had no idea.

Calista offered Daniel a sly smile. "If you won't tell me about the novel, tell me more about your new friends."

"They're like family." Hopefully, his tone made it clear that this was all he had to say. "My personal life isn't relevant."

Calista surprised him with a sudden laugh. "As an author, everything about you is very relevant. It affects the ways in which we promote you, how available you are for book tours and television spots, even various publicity angles."

All true, but it was clear to Daniel that it was only Jenna who really interested her.

"I'm not talking about Jenna with you."

Calista studied him for a long moment, then rose with an elegant grace. "We can table this discussion for now."

"I'm sorry you made this trip for nothing." Daniel stood. "Have a safe drive back."

Calista laughed. "I'm not returning. I'll be staying and enjoying your lovely community for a day or two."

"You're welcome to stay here." Daniel didn't want to offer, but he knew it was the right thing to do.

"I appreciate the kind offer, but I've already booked a suite at the GraceTown Inn."

"It's a lovely inn, right off the River Walk," he told her. "You'll like it."

"I'm sure I will." Calista's tone turned brisk. "Does noon work for you?"

"For what?"

"A lunch meeting." Calista flashed a smile. "While I'm in town, I have a preliminary marketing plan I'd like to go over with you."

CHAPTER TWENTY

Right at noon, Daniel arrived at Inner Biscuit, a café known for serving only breakfast and lunch. The harried young man at the host stand told him there was a thirty-minute wait. Just when Daniel was about to pull out his phone and text Calista, he spotted her at a table by the window

She caught his eye and waved him over.

Once Daniel was seated, the waiter arrived, but Calista shook her head. "Give us a few minutes. I'll signal when we're ready to order."

"What's going on, Calista? You've got that cat-swallowed-the-canary look." Daniel sat back in his seat.

"Why didn't you just tell me?" Her blue eyes snapped with excitement. "You know I've been wanting you to write true crime for years."

"What are you talking about?"

"The whole Michael Menard thing."

At Daniel's obviously blank look, Calista continued. "You know, the assault and jewel theft involving a prominent Philadelphia city councilmember."

"Why would you think I'd know anything about some guy on

the Philadelphia City Council? Frankly, I'm still trying to figure out what this has to do with me."

"I see what you're doing here." Calista's lips curved in an approving smile. "A woman accused of a crime by a wealthy and influential man assaults him, runs off with his family's priceless jewels and disappears from sight. She turns up in a quaint town in Maryland—"

"You're not making sense."

Calista continued as if he hadn't said a word. "You're obviously getting close to her to get the inside scoop, not only about the crime, but a glimpse into her mind. This is pure genius."

She opened her mouth to continue, but Daniel held up a hand.

"Calista, stop. You need to tell me what woman you are talking about."

"Jenna, of course."

Daniel laughed. "Jenna wouldn't pick up a dime off the sidewalk if it wasn't hers."

"The stolen jewels are worth a helluva lot more than a dime. The first theft netted her over a hundred thousand dollars. This last attempt, if it had succeeded, would have been even more. There was a witness and—"

"Calista, look, I know you're mad about the book being late and about the way we broke up—"

Calista rolled her eyes. "Writers and their egos. Yes, I'm annoyed about the book being late, but I broke up with you, remember?" She paused as a waiter walked past with a tray of drinks for another table. "Stop being coy, Daniel. You say Jenna couldn't do these things. Fine. Is that your angle for the book? What about evidence to the contrary? What's her side of the story?"

Daniel remained silent. He realized suddenly that he didn't even know the name of Jenna's former employer. Then he realized just as quickly that it didn't matter.

Calista leaned back in her seat. "You're serious that this isn't the book?"

Daniel nodded. "That's what I keep telling you."

"And she hasn't told you anything about this at all, has she?"

"I have no idea what you're talking about, Calista."

"Daniel, what are you thinking? Forget being worried about the book. I'm worried about *you*. Do you really not know who the woman living in your house is?"

Daniel was on the verge of snapping, *Of course I know her*, but he couldn't deny there were still a lot of question marks when it came to Jenna. Still, he had no intention of sharing that with Calista. "Where did you get this information that you think is so reliable?"

"Remember Bill?"

"The editor you hate?"

"That's the one." Calista waved an airy hand. "Anyway, after our editorial meeting last week, Bill brings up this scandal going on in Philadelphia where he's from. His mom is connected to the family, some 'society' thing. Anyway, he thought it would make an amazing true-crime story."

Daniel simply stared.

"Picture this." Calista made a frame with her hands. "Local politician eyeing a mayoral bid becomes embroiled in a scandal when the pretty private nurse he employed to take care of his sick wife—who happens to be part of one of Philadelphia's oldest families—attacks him and steals a bunch of her jewels."

"Still don't get it."

"Daniel, that nurse's name is Jenna Woodsen."

"No, Calista, just no. If that is the woman's name, then it's another Jenna Woodsen."

"C'mon, Daniel, you told me she's from Philadelphia and that she's a nurse." Calista lifted the cup of coffee to her lips. "There are also reputable eye witnesses."

Daniel had known all along that Jenna was hiding something,

but he'd thought it had been a bad breakup or maybe a crazy ex-boyfriend.

He did not for one second believe that Jenna, the woman he loved, the woman he'd come to know so well over the past couple of months, could be involved in an assault and a robbery.

"Surely you've googled her?"

The look on his face must have given Calista the answer, because her eyes widened. "You're kidding me."

"I don't pry into the lives of the women I date, and I'm not prying into Jenna's. If it's important, she'll tell me."

Calista laughed. "Honestly, Daniel, I thought you wrote fiction, not lived it."

Standing in the shade of the angel statue in the square, Jenna saw Violet approach. She made no move to leave. What would be the point? Though she didn't know for certain, she felt fairly sure that an angel could find a person hiding under a bed.

"The likeness really is remarkable," Jenna murmured as Violet moved to stand beside her.

"The stonemason used William's sketches of me to do the face."

"Did they know you're a real angel?"

"Naw, they simply saw someone who came to them in their hour of need." Violet gazed up at the statue. "I like to think she's a symbol of all good-hearted people who step up to help in a time of need."

"Hey, if they want to give you props, you should go with it."

Violet laughed, then wrapped her arm around Jenna's and gave it a squeeze. "I'm going to really miss you."

"You're the only friend I have." Jenna spoke in a light tone, only half joking.

"You know that's not true."

"I believe, in time, Rosemary will understand and forgive." Jenna's heart twisted. "But Daniel, he's going to be angry and hurt for a long, long time."

"He'll be hurt that you didn't feel you could trust him with the truth."

"I wanted to, but I couldn't."

Violet inclined her head, and the doubting look in those blue eyes had Jenna doubling down. "I couldn't."

With the hand that she'd wrapped around Jenna's arm, Violet began to gently stroke up and down, up and down.

Violet's tone remained easy. "I'm sure you do want to protect Daniel."

"I do." Jenna's voice grew strident. "I love him."

"The thing is, Daniel is a man, not a boy in need of protection." Violet brought a finger to her lips and studied Jenna for a long moment. "You could have told him the truth a long time ago, but you wanted to protect the relationship you were building. You didn't want to risk it."

Jenna brushed away the tears that wanted to fall. "That may have been part of it, but not all."

"Like I said, you could have told him the truth a long time ago, but you wanted to protect the relationship you were building. You didn't want to risk it."

Jenna turned her face away from Violet's discerning gaze. After a moment, she gave a jerky nod. "That may have been part of it, but not all."

"It's time to be the woman you are deep inside. Strong and courageous and able to overcome any obstacle tossed in your path."

"I need to go back?"

"Are you asking if you need to go back to Philadelphia or to Daniel?"

"Both."

Violet smiled. "Why ask the question when you already know the answer?"

∼

The house was silent when Jenna returned home. She felt shaken after her conversation with the officer at the Philadelphia PD, but relieved to have it over with.

Determined to retrieve the letters she'd left in the holder, Jenna headed straight for the sitting room. But instead of three envelopes, there were only two.

One addressed to Rosemary and one to Violet.

Jenna frowned as her heart gave a solid thump. "It has to be here—"

"Is this what you're looking for?"

Whirling, Jenna saw Daniel in the doorway, the opened envelope and letter in his hand.

"You read it?"

He nodded, then motioned for her to take a seat on the sofa.

When she did, he sat beside her.

She recalled the night she'd nearly sat on his lap and almost smiled. How she would give anything to be sitting there with his arms around her now.

"They're not going to get away with it," he said in a fierce tone, his eyes blazing.

"Who?"

"Menard, his assistant and whoever else is involved in trying to pin a crime on you that you didn't commit." Daniel's lips pressed together for a second. "And he's going to pay for attacking you."

Jenna blinked. "You believe me?"

"Of course I believe you." He shook his head. "I told Calista you wouldn't steal."

"Wait. Whoa." Jenna raised a hand. "Why were you talking about me with Calista?"

"I guess I need to back up." Daniel took a breath and appeared to steady. He gave Jenna a summary of what Calista had told him.

Jenna opened her mouth, but Daniel continued. "Before she left this morning, she asked where you're from, what you do for a living. I told her you're a nurse from Philadelphia. She made the leap."

"That's a pretty big leap."

"Calista is a big-picture gal. It's part of the reason she's such a great editor. Anyway, she got it in her head that I was working on a true-crime novel in which you play a part." Daniel chuckled, then sobered. "I made it very clear that not only is there no true-crime novel in the works, but if you are the Jenna Woodsen the police want to question, you are innocent."

"When did you have this discussion?"

"Over lunch."

"But that would have been before you read my letter." Jenna searched his face. "Before I gave you all the details and my side of the story."

"I didn't need details to know you are innocent." He took her hand, and she curled her fingers around his. "I know you."

Jenna swallowed past the lump that had lodged in her throat and fought to find her voice.

"I was so worried the police would come down on you for harboring a fugitive. That you'd lose your license to practice law, all because of me. That you wouldn't have the peace you came here looking for. And then there's my aunt. If she knew the truth, the stress on her heart would be too much. How could I have put her or you, any of you, through that?" She swiped at the tears streaming down her cheeks. "I don't know why I'm crying. I never cry."

"You've been carrying this worry alone." Understanding filled his green eyes, then his jaw set in a determined tilt. "You aren't alone any longer. We will fight these ridiculous assertions, and we will win."

"No, that's not it. I mean, it is, but…" Jenna shook her head and took a deep breath. "I'm saying we don't have to fight. I realized earlier today that I can't just keep running forever. So I called the Philadelphia PD." Jenna could still hear the deep sound of the police detective's voice.

"I spoke with an officer and told him I would come in and give my side of the story." An incredulous laugh escaped Jenna's lips. "He told me they had been looking for me not as a suspect, but for my safety. They charged Menard this morning with involvement in a multistate gambling ring and some other crimes, including sexual assault. His assistant is also facing charges."

"Are you serious? That's crazy." Daniel squeezed Jenna's hand. "But how did the story get out that an employee was suspected?"

"Oh, he tried to frame me for the theft, but the police never believed him. Apparently, they'd been quietly investigating him for a while. They didn't openly dispute his story because they didn't want to tip him off that they were on to him."

"Instead, they just let you live in fear? That's not fair."

The protectiveness in Daniel's voice warmed Jenna's heart.

"None of this is fair, Daniel. But it's over, mostly anyway, and that's what I care about. I gave my side of the story over the phone, but they'd like me to come in and give a statement in person."

His gaze searched her face. "I'd like to go with you, if you wouldn't mind."

"Thank you. That would mean a lot to me."

A cautious look crept into Daniel's eyes. "You said in your letter you were leaving GraceTown and wouldn't be back."

Jenna nodded. "That was the plan, but I couldn't do it. I couldn't leave you, Daniel. I couldn't leave Rosemary. I ran into Violet in the town square, and we talked. When I left her, I called the police department." Jenna glanced at the sheet of paper in his hand. "I was going to retrieve the letters, then speak with you and Rosemary in person."

Daniel inclined his head. "To tell us face-to-face what you revealed in the letters?"

"Yes, and to tell you I'm going to stay and fight." Her gaze met his. "Some things are worth fighting for, like you and the life I want to build with you. If you still want—"

The letter and the envelope slipped from his fingers and fluttered unnoticed to the floor.

His arms were around her now, and he was kissing her, and she was kissing him back with all the love in her heart.

"Second chances," she murmured as they came up for air.

Gently, oh so gently, he pushed a strand of hair back from her face. "What did you say, my darling?"

"We've been given a second chance, and I'm not going to waste a second of it."

EPILOGUE

Jenna brought a finger to her lips and watched Daniel finish hanging the last of three framed sketches. She'd supervised while he'd arranged them on the wall in the sitting area she thought of as their private refuge.

"How does that look?" Daniel stepped back and shot her a questioning glance.

Her answer came out on a breath, "Perfect."

The sketches were ones they'd found of Florence and Violet. The detail amazed them both. A pitcher filled with daisies on the bedside table. Lace curtains at the window fluttering in the breeze from a barely open window. A cotton blanket carefully folded at the bottom of Florence's bed while she slept.

"The sight of the cloth pressed against Florence's brow reminds me of you." Reaching over, Daniel took her hand and squeezed. "I remember how you nursed me back to health."

"So much love in these sketches," Jenna murmured.

In the one where Violet steadied Florence as she helped her drink from a glass, you couldn't see Violet's face, only a side view of a slender young nurse, her hair coming loose from her cap to spill against her cheek.

Jenna's favorite of the three sketches they'd chosen to frame was the one in which Violet held an armful of fresh bedding and had a weary—but relieved—smile on her face.

"The Angel of GraceTown." Daniel slung an arm around Jenna's shoulders. "She blessed this town in its hour of need."

"She will never be forgotten," Jenna added, recalling the inscription.

"Certainly not by us."

"No," Jenna agreed. "Not by us."

It had been difficult for Jenna to watch Violet walk out the door several days earlier, not knowing when or if they'd ever see her again.

As if Daniel sensed her happy mood was rapidly fading, he took her hand and tugged her toward the door. "Let's check out the garden."

"Right now?"

He smiled. "I can't think of a better time."

Perhaps it was only Jenna's imagination, but the sun seemed to shine extra bright over the area. After taking a seat on the bench, they sat for several seconds in silence, struck by the bounty before them. Plump red tomatoes, dark green zucchini and fat pumpkins. Vegetables and fruits that shouldn't be ready to pick and eat this early in the summer, but somehow were.

Jenna inhaled deeply, loving how the scents of the various herbs mingled with the sweet floral fragrances wafting from the many blooming plants.

She watched Daniel's lips quirk upward when his gaze settled on the lemon tree, its branches heavy with fruit.

"Rosemary has done an outstanding job taking care of the garden since Violet left." Daniel turned to Jenna. "Where is she this afternoon, anyway?"

"With Barry." Jenna smiled. "Where else?"

"Figures." Daniel chuckled, then his gaze settled on the strawberry patch. "This garden is amazing. I can't believe we haven't made time to come out here in almost a month."

"You've been busy revising. I didn't realize edits took so long."

"Three weeks isn't long at all."

"Well, I thought your story was perfect just the way it was." Daniel had let her read the manuscript before he'd sent it to Calista, and Jenna had been blown away. It was evident, at least to her, that he'd put his heart and soul into it.

"I didn't think you could make me love this one more than your first. But you did." Jenna paused and tried to put into words how his latest story had made her feel. "The themes of resilience and second chances really spoke to my heart."

Daniel reached over and took her hand. "Being here, with the three of you, changed me. That came through in my writing."

Her gaze locked with his. "You changed me as well."

As he brought their joined hands to his mouth and placed a kiss on her knuckles, the sight of the glittering diamond on her left hand had her lips curving upward. She loved her ring and the man who had given it to her.

When Daniel had proposed and snapped the ring box open to reveal the marquis-cut diamond nestled inside, Jenna had said yes. To the proposal, to the ring he'd slipped on her finger and to the promise of forever.

Now, they were planning a wedding. Rosemary half-jokingly had said maybe they should make it a double, leading Jenna to believe a proposal from Barry might be on the horizon.

The thought that her aunt had also found happiness in this town filled her with satisfaction and joy.

"We should grab a late lunch," Daniel suggested. "Maybe stop in at the Black Apron. You can show Ted your ring."

"I told him the last time all I needed was a gold band and love." Jenna smiled, remembering that day. "That's still true, though I adore my ring."

"I love seeing you wear it, knowing the promise behind it."

Leaning over, he kissed her.

Wrapping her arms around him, she kissed him back, until they were both out of breath and laughing.

"I often think that if it hadn't been for Violet, I never would have come here, never would have met you—"

"I believe we were meant to be together, and that somehow, some way, it would have happened."

Jenna thought of the girl who'd so quickly become a part of her family. "I can't believe how easily Rosemary accepted that Violet is an angel."

"When Violet said she wanted to tell Rosemary personally, I wondered how your aunt would react."

"Rosemary said Violet was always an angel in her eyes anyway."

They both smiled at that.

When Jenna had asked Violet where she was headed several days ago, Violet had said only that she was going to a place where she was needed.

"Most people seem to accept the story that Violet is traveling the world for the summer before she heads off to college."

"Maybe by the time they start asking again, we can distract them with news of a baby." Daniel wiggled his eyebrows and made her laugh, even as her heart gave a quick leap at the thought. Then his expression turned serious. "Do you think she'll show up for the wedding?"

Jenna thought of the angel she loved like a sister, and her tone turned wistful. "I guess it just depends on which way the wind blows. One thing is certain."

Daniel brushed a lock of hair back from Jenna's face with a gentle finger. "What's that?"

"Wherever she is, once it comes time for her to leave, they'll never forget her."

～

I hope you enjoyed reading THE ANGEL IN THE SQUARE. I have to admit the GraceTown series is a favorite of mine. I know you will love all the books set in the town known for unexplainable happenings. Even though each story can standalone, you will see friends from other books in the series pop up every now and then…which is always so much fun!

Coming in March 2024 is THE ENCHANTED MUSIC BOX, a story you're going to absolutely adore.

Aided by an enchanted music box a young woman learns valuable lessons about life and love as she sees her life as it was, as it is and, as it could be.

This is one you really won't want to miss, so reserve your copy of The Enchanted Music Box today!

If you haven't yet read THE PINK HOUSE, book 1 in the GraceTown series, you're in for a treat. Grab your copy now or keep reading for a sneak peek:

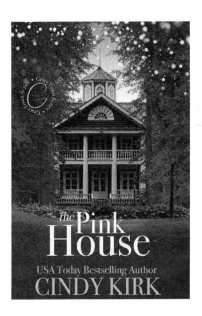

SNEAK PEEK OF THE PINK HOUSE

Chapter 1

"Pack it, or smash it?" Standing in the middle of a room full of boxes, Hannah Danbury lifted one hand palm up then the other as she weighed the options.

Her BFF, Emma Sands, held the mug sporting the logo of Hannah's former employer between two fingers, a look of distaste on her face. "I vote smash it."

Though tempted, Hannah shook her head. "If I did smash it, I'd be the one cleaning up the mess. Not worth it."

"Please don't tell me you're going to keep it. Not after what they did to you."

Hannah hesitated for only an instant. "It's a good mug, but not for me. Put it in the donate pile."

Emma offered a reluctant nod as Hannah continued to drop utensils into a box labeled Kitchen Stuff.

"You gave that company over eight years of your life." Emma's lips pursed. "Don't tell me they couldn't have found a place for you when they restructured."

The thought had crossed Hannah's mind a dozen times, but

ruminating on her dismissal served no purpose. She hadn't been the only one let go when the company had been sold. A lot of really good employees had found themselves without jobs.

"Layoffs happen." That was Hannah's go-to phrase whenever anyone had expressed sympathy during the past eight weeks. "Restructuring is part of corporate life nowadays."

"True, but they don't usually happen when you're still grieving for…" Her voice trailed off, and sympathy filled Emma's brown eyes.

"Brian. You can say his name, Ems. I don't forget he's gone just because we don't talk about him." Last year, Hannah's formerly healthy husband had been diagnosed with cancer only months before his thirtieth birthday. He'd died six weeks later. "Brian is always with me. I look around this apartment and see him everywhere. It breaks my heart to think of all the dreams we had—he had—that will never come true."

"Let's take a break." Emma set the mug on the island counter and gestured toward the sofa. "Is that the real reason you're leaving Greensboro? To get away from the memories?"

Hannah stepped around several boxes to drop onto the sofa. She had asked herself the same question Emma was asking.

"If I was still employed at Mingus, I'd stay. With no income and my dad's house in GraceTown falling into my lap…" Hannah shrugged. "Seems like the perfect time to return home."

"I'm happy for you, I really am, but I'm sad for me. I wish home wasn't Maryland." Emma grabbed two sodas from the refrigerator. After handing one can to Hannah, she took a seat beside her friend on the sofa. "I mean, GraceTown is adorable, but it's not like it's down the block."

Hannah reached over and gave her friend's hand a squeeze. "I'm going to miss you, too. Big-time."

They sipped their sodas in companionable silence before Emma shifted to face Hannah. "I've never asked. I mean, I know your dad won't be there, but what about Brian's parents? Do they still live in GraceTown?"

Hannah nodded. "They do, but I doubt I'll see much of them. Brian's sister, Katie, and her new husband are in town, and Katie and her mom are close."

Hannah had liked her in-laws well enough. With her own mother passing away when she was small, she'd hoped to forge a closeness with Debbie. That connection had never materialized.

"In a way, with your dad and stepmom already in Florida, it's like you're moving to a completely new town."

"I suppose." Hannah lifted the can of soda, but didn't take a drink. "Except I did grow up there."

Emma pushed silky brown hair back from her heart-shaped face with the back of her hand, the gesture as elegant as the woman herself. "Are you going to look for another marketing position once you get settled?"

This wasn't the first time Emma had broached the topic of Hannah resuming her career. Like Hannah had once been, Emma was all about opportunities and advancement. Each time before when Emma had asked, Hannah had simply told her the truth—she wasn't sure what she would do.

Since she knew Emma worried, Hannah brought up a possibility that had recently surfaced, one she found intriguing. "Mackenna, she's a friend from way back, works at Collister College. We've stayed in touch through the years, mostly online. She mentioned they have a position in marketing and student recruitment coming open in September. She thinks I'd be a fabulous candidate and offered to put in a good word."

"September is four months away." Emma lowered her soda. "Do you really want to wait that long? Plus, there's no guarantee you'd get the job."

"I know that." Hannah kept her tone matter-of-fact. "But it sounds as if it could be a possibility."

In fact, it was the first position that had interested her, though she was sure the appeal was because she'd be working in the same area as Mackenna.

Thankfully, she had time to consider all her options. Brian had carried a robust life insurance policy, and Hannah had yet to touch any of the money. Between it and what she was making off the sale of the townhouse, she could easily take the summer off.

She told herself she deserved the break. It had been a tough year, with the past couple of months being the roughest. She'd lost her job, learned her dad was leaving GraceTown for sunny Florida, then she'd decided to put her own home on the market and move. The hits just kept coming with the first anniversary of Brian's death last week, six days before their thirtieth birthday.

When she and Brian had first started dating, sharing a birthday had seemed incredibly cool. Now that day would forever be a yearly reminder of all she'd lost.

"We thought we had all the time in the world." Hannah gazed out the window. "We had a plan. Our twenties would be focused on building our careers. The thirties, well, that was when we planned to start a family. Now here I am, turning thirty and making new plans alone."

"Speaking of birthdays." Emma placed a hand on Hannah's arm and gave it a sympathetic squeeze before rising. Hurrying across the room, she stopped where she'd dropped her stuff when she arrived. She returned to the sofa with a white bakery box.

Emma's eyes met hers. "I know you said you didn't want to go out and celebrate. But we're not going out, we're here."

A smile tugged at the corners of Hannah's lips. "What do you have in there?"

"It struck me that this could be the last time we'll be able to celebrate your birthday together." Carefully opening the bakery box, Emma removed a cupcake. "I say a birthday without cake is like sex without a man."

With its swirl of pink frosting dotted with tiny beads of white that resembled pearls and topped with a pink crown, the cupcake reminded Hannah of something out of a fairy tale.

A pretty bow of organza ribbon edged with pink satin encircled the base. Emma held out the gorgeous creation. "A cupcake worthy of a princess for a princess."

A lump formed in Hannah's throat. "It-it's gorgeous."

"It's from that new bakery out on Whittier." Emma pushed the cupcake at her when Hannah only stared. "The reviews say their cupcakes taste every bit as good as they look."

"Thank you, Ems." Tears stung the backs of Hannah's eyes at her friend's thoughtfulness. "You're going to have to help me eat it."

"No way am I making you share. Not on your birthday." Emma smiled and pulled another cupcake from the box. "That's why I got one for myself."

The laughter that bubbled up in Hannah was as precious a gift as the gorgeous cupcake and the beautiful friend beside her.

Three weeks later, Hannah moved into the only home she'd known before leaving for college at eighteen.

Though the house hadn't changed, GraceTown had continued to grow and now spread in all directions. Homes dotted ground where crops had once flourished.

Like the hardworking people who inhabited these homes, the houses in Hannah's neighborhood remained untouched by the passage of time. In the block she considered her own, the homes were older and boasted two stories and large front porches. Blankets of lush green grass and flowering bushes spoke to the pride of ownership.

Many of the neighbors were the same. Sean O'Malley from down the street had a ladder resting against the trunk of a large pin oak as he sawed off a limb.

Geraldine Walker and Beverly Raymond still lived across the street.

In their early seventies, with hair now sporting more gray than brown, the two women waved from their porch swing as she drove by.

As Hannah waved back and called out a greeting through her open car window, she realized just how much she was looking forward to living in a neighborhood again.

The townhouse she and Brian had purchased right after college had been located in an area of Greensboro, North Carolina, called Friendly West. They'd been happy in the area inhabited by mostly young professionals, men and women focused on their careers and more interested in their own personal activities than socializing with neighbors.

She understood the focus. She and Brian had embraced that same lifestyle, working long hours, then filling any free hours with time spent together.

Hannah hoped to do things differently this time. While she would always give a job her best, never again would she let a career consume her life.

Though she'd meant what she'd said to Emma about under-standing that layoffs happen, it still hurt to be cast aside after eight years of unwavering loyalty.

Hannah shoved the thought aside. She would not bring old regrets into her new life.

After setting a box of kitchen items on the counter, Hannah returned to her vehicle. Thankfully, her father had left most of his furniture, which had saved her the cost of moving hers.

Though she had to admit that parting with the sofa, chairs and bedroom furniture she and Brian had chosen together had been more difficult than she'd imagined.

Each piece had been purchased after much consideration and debate. She remembered one spirited discussion that had ended with them making love on the floor where their new sofa would eventually sit. Afterward, relaxed and sated, they'd come to a meeting of the minds on fabric.

Hannah's hand stilled on a box of dishes, the memory bittersweet. Brian had been so healthy, so fit, so incredibly vibrant and alive…until he wasn't.

"Need help?"

The unexpected voice had Hannah whirling, nearly hitting her head on the side of the hatch of her car. She blinked and realized this was no stranger offering assistance. This man was someone she knew. "Charlie?"

"Hey, you remember." He flashed an easy grin that was as much a part of him as the worn jeans and the dark wavy hair that went past his collar.

"How could I forget?" Her tone turned droll. "You were in our wedding."

Not just *in* the wedding. He'd been Brian's best man. Their friendship had been one Hannah had never understood.

While her husband and Charlie had both been popular athletes and good-looking guys in high school, Charlie had struck her as over-the-top loud and something of a show-off.

Brian had always told her that if she took the time to get to know Charlie, she'd like him. There had never been an opportunity. The two boys had gone to different colleges, and after graduation, she and Brian had married and settled in Greensboro.

"I'm sorry I couldn't make the funeral." Charlie shifted from one foot to the other. "My mom was in the hospital and pretty sick. With my dad out of the picture, I needed to stay close."

"I understand." Those days were a blur anyway. Besides, Charlie had always struck her as a wildcard, and she hadn't needed any drama at the service. There had been enough with Brian's mother fainting and hitting her head, necessitating a 911 call.

Hannah remembered wishing she could just give in to her

grief, weep uncontrollably and fall apart, leaving someone else to pick up the pieces.

Instead, she'd gone on autopilot and made the arrangements, contacted everyone who needed to be reached and comforted Brian's parents.

Only in her townhouse, once everyone had left and all the duties were done, had it hit her. Brian, with his laughing hazel eyes and bright smile, would never again kiss her, hold her or call her Hannah Banana. All the dreams she'd had for the future had died with him.

"Hannah." Charlie's tone gentled. "You okay?"

How many times during the past year had she been asked that same question? Fifty? A hundred?

She'd discovered there was only one suitable answer, preferably accompanied by a slight smile.

"I'm fine." Taking in a breath, she expelled it slowly. "Or I will be once I get all this stuff unloaded and inside."

"I'll help." Charlie didn't wait for a response. He simply scooped up a box containing wedding china and hefted it as easily as if it held feathers.

"Thanks." Hannah grabbed a box of her own and followed him into the house.

"Where do you want this?" he asked.

For a second, she considered telling him to just set it down in the living room, but she knew she'd have to eventually move it. "Would you mind putting it on the dining room table?"

"No problem." He set the box on a table that sported a thin layer of dust.

Hannah stood there for a moment, studying the mahogany table and matching china hutch, relics of a bygone era. She'd want to update, that much was certain. But until she had a clear vision of how she wanted to update the interior, she'd put what was here to good use.

"Your father thought about taking these pieces with him to Florida, but Sandie was having none of it."

Sandie, whom her father had married last year, had very definite ideas. Her dad appeared to take the woman's bossiness in stride. Hannah figured he must see something in her. After nearly thirty years as a widower, he'd finally taken the plunge.

"In this instance, I agree with Sandie. Leaving them behind made sense. The pieces are heavy and would have cost a fortune to move." Hannah shook her head. "Plus, I've seen pictures of their Florida home. These wouldn't fit in at all."

"Your dad still had a hard time walking away." Charlie's sharp-eyed gaze surveyed the dated decor. "He told me it felt like he was leaving a part of himself behind."

Hannah understood. She'd felt the same about her furniture in Greensboro.

"What else did my dad tell you?" Hannah hadn't even known that Charlie and her father were that well acquainted.

"That knowing you'd be living here was a comfort."

Now, this was getting weird. Hannah lifted a hand. "Tell me again how you know my father."

Surprise skittered across Charlie's face. "Neighbors talk."

"Neighbors? You don't live around here." Hannah struggled to recall just where Charlie lived, then decided the mental gymnastics weren't worth the effort. That had been high school. Undoubtedly, he'd moved numerous times since then.

"My mom and I live next door." He jerked his head toward the north. "We moved in last year."

"You live with your mother?"

Charlie arched a dark brow. "You have a problem with that?"

"Nope." Hannah wasn't surprised, not really. Just like she hadn't been surprised when Brian had told her that Charlie had dropped out of the engineering program at MIT after two years. Brian said it was because Charlie was so smart he was bored.

Hannah suspected too much partying. "Listen, you don't have to help me."

He grinned. "What box do you want brought in next?"

With Charlie's help, they emptied the back of her car in short order.

As she watched him carry box after box, Hannah had to admit that Charlie had retained his youthful good looks. His hair was still glossy, thick and dark and his body as muscular and lean as it had been during his football days.

Either he worked out regularly, or his day job involved a lot of lifting, because he had no problem handling any of the boxes, even ones she'd overfilled.

"That's the last." He set the box where she'd instructed in the main-floor bedroom. "Anything else I can help with?"

"No, thank you." This time, Hannah's smile came easy. "You've been very helpful."

"Brian was my friend. You're my neighbor." He cleared his throat. "If you ever need anything—"

He lifted a marker from the table and wrote a phone number on the top of the nearest box. "Call anytime, or stop over. I'm right next door."

With a wink, he turned and strode out the door.

Hannah glanced at the number, but made no move to add it to her phone. Instead, she began unpacking, determined to put the past behind her and start a new life.

Without Brian.

See why readers rave about THE PINK HOUSE. Pick up your copy today!

ALSO BY CINDY KIRK

Good Hope Series

The Good Hope series is a must-read for those who love stories that uplift and bring a smile to your face.

GraceTown Series

Enchanting stories that are a perfect mixture of romance, friendship, and magical moments set in a community known for unexplainable happenings.

Hazel Green Series

These heartwarming stories, set in the tight-knit community of Hazel Green, are sure to move you, uplift you, inspire and delight you. Enjoy uplifting romances that will keep you turning the page!

Holly Pointe Series

Readers say "If you are looking for a festive, romantic read this Christmas, these are the books for you."

Jackson Hole Series

Heartwarming and uplifting stories set in beautiful Jackson Hole, Wyoming.

Silver Creek Series

Engaging and heartfelt romances centered around two powerful families whose fortunes were forged in the Colorado silver mines.

Sweet River Montana Series

A community serving up a slice of small-town Montana life, where helping hands abound and people fall in love in the context of home and family.

15262068R00140